Return
to the
Shadows

Return to the Shadows

A Jemimah Hodge Mystery

MARIE ROMERO CASH

Kenmore, WA

Epicenter Press
6524 NE 181st St.
Suite 2
Kenmore, WA 98028

www.epicenterpress.com
www.camelpress.com
www.coffeetownpress.com

For more information go to: www.marieromerocash.com

This is a work of fiction. Names, characters, places, brands, incidents, media, and incidents are either the product of the author's imagination or are used fictitiously. Any resemblance to actual persons living or dead, businesses, events or locales is entirely coincidental.

Cover design by Dawn Anderson

ISBN: 978-1-60381-989-3 (Trade Paper)
ISBN: 978-1-60381-815-5 (eBook)

Produced in the United States of America

Other Books in the Jemimah Hodge Series:
Shadows among the Ruins
Deadly Deception
Treasure among the Shadows
The Mariachi Murder

Chapter One

———•———

That Santa Fe pre-dawn Sunday morning Jamie Curry drove south on Highway 14. He whistled a tune as he anticipated spending most of the day in the Ortiz Mountain Range. It had been over a month since he had a day off from his job as chef for the Anasazi Hotel, and he was looking forward to spending that entire day hiking through the hills, taking in the fresh mountain air. As he settled back on the seat, he turned the A/C on low and slipped a CD into the player.

He marveled at the scenery around him. What he loved most about the Santa Fe area was that it was unlike any other place he had lived. There were no large bridges or waterways, no freeways or multi-storied buildings looming into the western sky; except, of course, for the Eldorado Hotel, a monolithic structure where he previously worked. He particularly liked the idea that he could drive from one end of the city to the other in fifteen minutes. He sighed. *I love my life.*

A few miles past the village of Cerrillos, some eighteen miles from Santa Fe, he took a left turn onto a rut-filled dirt road which led to a dead end at the base of a rocky outcropping. He parked the Subaru, reached in the back for his backpack and began his trek along a faded path. After a long hike up the side of the mountain, he stopped to rest under a grove of cottonwood trees. A narrow brook wound its way up ahead, its gentle meandering breaking into the quiet of the morning as the water rippled against the rocks. The sun had barely begun to peek over the mountain range. The air was invigorating, cool and crisp. Life didn't get any better than this.

He raised himself up and started up a rocky incline. When he reached the main trail, he felt his cell phone vibrate in his pocket.

"What?" he answered, with more intensity than he intended, annoyed that the call interrupted his communion with nature.

"Where are you, Jamie? We were supposed to meet for breakfast. It's almost seven."

He glanced at his watch. *Oh shit.* He had completely forgotten. "Sorry, I spaced it out. I'm working my way back to the car. I'll be there as soon as I can," he lied. He heard a long sigh.

"Forget it," she said. "By the time you get back here, I'll have already left for church. Let's just take a raincheck and catch up some other time."

Based on the sharp tone of her voice, he could tell she was pissed.

"I said I was sorry. Let me make it up to you. We can have dinner tonight at the hotel, and maybe catch a movie after?"

She thought about it for a minute. "All right. I didn't mean to jump down your throat, but I had been looking forward to seeing you all week."

He smiled. "Okay, I'll pick you up at seven."

He hung up and slipped the phone into his pocket, turning around to get his bearings, then he headed in a northwesterly direction. After about a mile, the terrain had turned rocky and then flattened out. He almost lost his footing stumbling over a dry root and reached out to balance himself on a nearby tree. Up ahead was an area marked with a No Trespassing sign strung to a barbed wire fence. He figured it might be part of an old Indian ruin he noticed on the map when looking for a hiking place.

After another long period of walking along the trail, he looked at the time and decided to call it a day. Looking around, he figured if he cut across in a southerly direction, it would be a shorter path to his car. A hundred yards in, he spotted a sleeping bag under a clump of bushes and thought it odd that someone would leave their camping gear out in this remote area. He continued going straight in his intended direction, which would walk him next to the campsite.

Unsure of what he was looking at up ahead, he squinted his eyes to focus as he walked. He was a few yards from the campsite when his knees buckled beneath him. He gasped when he saw a bloody arm sticking out from under the bag. "*Jesus God Almighty*," he bellowed. His voice echoed through the canyon. He turned and tore off in the direction of his vehicle. By the time he spotted it up ahead, his breath was coming in short gulps. His hands were shaking so violently he couldn't unlock the door of the SUV. Jamie Curry had no desire to return to what he had seen as he grabbed his cell phone from his pocket and dialed 911, his weak voice barely able to get the words out. The magnificent sunrise developing around him escaped his notice.

Chapter Two

Saturday, the previous day

THE SKY OVER Santa Fe was as deep a blue as it had ever been in early May. Multi-colored wildflowers covered the grassy knoll at the base of the Sangre de Cristo Mountains overlooking Santa Fe. A gentle breeze whisked up a handful of rose petals and shuffled them across the grounds of Bishop's Lodge, five miles from Santa Fe, and deposited them at the door of the historic chapel built in 1860 by French Bishop Jean Baptiste Lamy. A small crowd milled around, exchanging pleasantries. The ancient chapel bell began to toll its dulcet tones and a distinguished looking usher dressed in a dark suit motioned to the attendees that the ceremony was about to begin.

Because the tiny chapel could only accommodate a small group, the couple took their places under a canopy in the center of the patio as the strains of their favorite song, "I Always Get Lucky With You", echoed through the stillness. The bride was attired in a simple but elegant white dress suit, her honey-blonde hair styled in a fashionable upsweep secured with a turquoise and silver barrette. A small diamond heart on a gold chain circled her neck, accentuated by matching earrings, both gifts from the groom. The groom wore a dark suit jacket over a crisp white shirt and a pair of indigo denim jeans. His cowboy boots were newly polished. The two were a striking couple.

The priest, clad in a cream-colored chasuble with Our Lady of Guadalupe embroidered on the front panel, motioned for the crowd to be seated. The onlookers hushed in anticipation as he cleared his throat and smiled. Tim McCabe walked the bride up the cobblestone path and handed her over to the groom.

"I know this is preaching to the choir," the pastor said, "but I make it a practice to inquire if anyone present has any objection to the union of this couple. If so, speak your piece." In a melodramatic movement, his gaze swept across the crowd. He clapped his hands and chuckled. "Well, then, let's get these two married!"

He joined the couple's hands and blessed them. "I've known this guy since he was a little kid. There is not a more honest, decent person present in this crowd. He has walked alongside this beautiful woman for a number of years, and it is time they are united in Holy Matrimony." He placed his hand over their joined hands.

"Rick Romero, do you take this woman as your soulmate, to cherish and love her for all eternity?"

His eyes met hers. "Yes, I do."

"And do you, Jemimah Hodge, take this man as your eternal soulmate, to cherish and love, through thick and thin, as long as you both shall live?" The priest laughed. "I threw in those extra promises because I know this guy pretty well and you might get more than what you bargained for."

She grinned and squeezed his hand. "Yes, I do."

The couple exchanged custom-made lapis encrusted gold bands, smiled broadly at each other, and turned to face the pastor.

"By the powers vested in me by the Church and the great State of New Mexico, I now pronounce you husband and wife,

wife and husband. It is my wish that each day of your married life overflows with love and abundance." He turned to Rick. "You may kiss your beautiful bride."

And there it was, the phrase that spurred the crowd to break into whistles, cheers and loud applause as the couple shared a long embrace. One by one, the guests came forward to offer their congratulations. The wedding party consisted of Rick's brother, Carlos, as best man, and Jemimah's assistant, Katie Gonzales, as maid of honor. Romero's secretary, Clarissa, Detectives Chacon and Martinez, Sheriff Medrano and a host of others surrounded the couple. Tim and Laura McCabe were the first in line. Carlos patted his brother on the back.

"I never thought you'd tie the knot before me, Rick. You're a very lucky man," he said.

"That I am, Carlos. Blessed in more ways than I can imagine. I'm glad you delayed your trip to Spain so you could be here."

"Miss your wedding? No way, brother," he said. "I'll be taking off after the reception."

Rick's face lit up as Jemimah moved closer to him. He couldn't believe they were finally married. She kissed him lightly on the lips.

"No turning back, Detective," she smiled.

"Not a chance, Doctor H. I'm in it for the duration."

"As am I, *querido.*"

He chuckled as he lifted her up and twirled her around. "Did I just hear you call me *querido?* I see you've been brushing up on your Spanish."

"Well, if we're going to be honeymooning in Mexico, I want to be sure all them *señoritas* know you're off limits."

He squeezed her shoulders. "I promise I won't let you out of my sight, *mi amor.*"

Chapter Three

Sunday morning.

RICK AND JEMIMAH were preparing to drive to Albuquerque International Airport to catch a nine o'clock morning flight to Mexico City, where they were looking forward to a glorious week on the beaches of Acapulco. As he reached down to grab the suitcases, the cell phone on the counter vibrated.

"Don't answer that," Jemimah said. "We need to get on the road."

Too late. Romero had just picked it up. It was Sheriff Medrano.

"Rick, I know this is a bad time, but you need to put that honeymoon on the back burner. We just got a call in about a body out there in Cerrillos," he said.

Romero flinched. "Oh, come on, Eddie. We're on our way out. You can't do this to us. Let State Police handle it. New Mexico law gives them equal jurisdiction."

"I'm well aware of that," the Sheriff said. "But the DA's pressing us to not let that happen. Politics play a big hand in law enforcement, you know that."

"Still...," Romero said.

"You don't know how sorry I am, Rick, but we're shorthanded. I gotta call in my boss card. You'll just have to postpone for a few days, and when the rest of the guys return from training, you can take off. Sorry to do this to you, *hombre,* but there's no other choice." He gave Romero the particulars. "I've already called in a ten-zero-one, our third homicide of the year. The crime scene unit and the Medical Examiner will probably be on hand by the time you get there."

Romero repeated his protest, but the Sheriff had already hung up the call. He slammed his phone on the counter. "Son of a bitch!" He pushed the suitcases aside and looked at Jemimah.

She dropped her handbag on the counter. "Don't tell me. That was Sheriff Medrano. I can tell by the look on your face it's not good news."

"I'm so sorry, Sweetie. I couldn't talk my way out of it." He explained the details to her, and retrieved his holster and weapon from the closet. "I don't know how long this is going to take, but I'll give you a call first chance I get." He reached over and kissed her. "We'll get there, I promise."

He pushed the porch door open and walked to his cruiser. He could feel Jemimah's eyes following him, but he knew she was well aware of what his job as a Sheriff's deputy entailed, like it or not. He didn't need to tell her she couldn't accompany him this time, since she was technically no longer employed by the County. There was a rule in place that didn't allow husbands and wives to be employed together in law enforcement, and their decision to marry put the rule into play.

Romero pulled out of the driveway of Jemimah's ranch onto Highway 14. According to Medrano, the scene of the crime was about ten miles south, before the turnoff to Madrid. He wished he'd passed up the sheriff's call, but better here than when they were at the airport. As he pointed the cruiser east onto the dirt road, the familiar sound of his radio crackling filled the cab. The dispatcher relayed information about an abandoned vehicle on a trail just east of Highway 14 and added she was checking the tag number. He could hear the clicking of her keyboard as he drove along. He put the cruiser in second gear as the road up ahead became rough and bumpy. The dispatcher's voice came on again.

"Detective Romero, I'll have to get back to you. It appears to be a rental car and I need to check with the company to get the particulars."

Romero thanked her and continued on the road, which he recognized as a short distance from the periphery of Tim McCabe's Indian ruins on San Lazaro Pueblo, an area he was definitely familiar with. Up ahead, he saw the coroner's van parked next to the crime techs' vehicle. "Here we go," he said to himself as he pulled in alongside and killed the engine.

Chapter Four

D ETECTIVE ROMERO WALKED more than a mile across a grassy knoll along a trail which led to a large section of ground out in the open that had been cordoned off. The bright yellow tape stuck out like a sore thumb, a stark contrast to the peaceful serenity of the surroundings. He noticed how quiet it was, the only sounds the occasional chirp of a blue jay in the background.

Charlie Roberts looked up at him. "Hey, Detective. Thought you were off on a honeymoon somewhere with that pretty bride of yours?"

Romero grumbled. "Unfortunately, duty calls."

"Duty by the name of Sheriff Medrano, I take it? Damn, the guy could have given you a break," he said.

Romero knelt at his side. "Says it couldn't be avoided, so I'm cool with that. What's the story here?"

He pointed to the blue Subaru barely visible in the distance. "That guy was in the middle of an early morning hike around the area, and stumbled onto a body covered with a sleeping bag. Scared the crap out of him. I think he's calmed down enough to give you a statement."

Roberts pulled back the sleeping bag. The victim was

sprawled on the ground, eyes closed, mouth open, his arms splayed cruciform style. Romero looked at the gaping wound on the side of his head.

"Someone sure didn't like this guy," he said as he inspected the body. The blood had soaked into the grass around the victim and onto his shirtsleeve. His head was turned to one side and it was pretty obvious he had been shot. A wound about the size of a golf ball had peeled back the flesh on his left temple.

"Any I.D. on the guy?"

Roberts shook his head. "Not as far as I can see. Just got here about ten minutes ago. Waited for you to arrive. Been checking the scene for anything that might be out of synch. He's dressed in warmups and hiking shoes, so he might have been doing the same thing as the guy who found him. This is a fairly nice out-of-the-way area for a hike," he said. "Been here myself a few times."

Romero looked down at the victim's shoes and noticed they had a sticky residue on the soles and pine needles embedded in the indentations. "Get those shoes to the Crime Lab and see what that is."

"Will do. I'll get you a copy of the lab report once it's in."

Romero saw the Medical Examiner's crew heading in his direction, loaded down with metal cases and a gurney. "While the ME does his job, I'll have a talk with our witness and get him on his way."

He trudged across the road and back to the clearing where Jamie Curry looked up as he approached. His face was pale and his hands were shaking. Romero introduced himself.

"I need to ask you a few questions, Jamie, and then I'll get you on your way. Not the kind of experience one likes to have on such a beautiful morning, hey?"

Curry forced a weak smile. "Definitely not my idea, either."

The witness gave Romero the details of his discovery. "I was about an hour and a half into my hike, getting ready to cut across through the gate on the adjoining lot. I tripped on a branch and almost toppled into the body. The guy was covered with a sleeping bag, his hand sticking out from under."

"How did you know he just wasn't sleeping?"

Curry took a deep breath. "Before I became a chef, I drove an ambulance for a medical center. From the color of his hand and what little blood I could see, I figured he was dead."

After a series of general questions, Romero was satisfied that Curry was an innocent bystander. "I'll get my notes transcribed and get in touch with you to come by the office and sign a witness statement. Meanwhile, you can continue on your way," he said.

"I don't think I have it in me to stay around here," he said. "I'm going to get my butt back to town."

Romero put out his hand. "You going to be okay? You're welcome to stick around here for a while."

Curry shook his head. "No thanks. I'll be okay once my heart rate gets back to normal. It's not zipping along like it was earlier."

Romero watched as Curry climbed into his vehicle. He returned to the scene and spent the next couple of hours looking for any clues that might have been left behind. He couldn't help but wonder about the victim. What was he doing there, what had occurred in his final moments? Did he know his assailant? Was he caught off guard? What happened? The thought crossed his mind that this fellow might have been one of the many treasure hunters who were out scouring the southwest looking for Tim McCabe's buried booty.

With the silence of the crime scene, he could feel the isolation and peace surrounding the area. No birds chirping, no coyotes howling. Tall pines and low junipers formed an uneasy circle around the site. By mid-afternoon, all Romero had was a cold-blooded murder with no apparent witnesses, motive or suspects.

As he signed off with the tech and the ME crew, he could see his hopes of getting on with the honeymoon rapidly fading away.

Chapter Five

IT WOULD BE four o'clock that afternoon by the time Romero stopped by his office before going back home. The substation was located off Main Street in the Village of Cerrillos. The oversized tires on the cruiser crunched noisily on the gravel driveway as he maneuvered his vehicle into the parking space in front of the building.

As he walked through the front door, Clarissa, his assistant, looked up at him, a surprised look on her face.

"Hey, Boss. I thought you'd be landing in Acapulco about this time. What happened? You guys get into an argument already?"

"Fortunately, no. Let's just say duty intervened."

Clarissa frowned. "Don't tell me. I assume that duty was prompted by Sheriff Medrano?"

"You assume correctly, but to his credit, he was backed against a wall and couldn't find his way around it. He would have had to call State Police in, and that would remove the case from our jurisdiction."

Clarissa rolled her eyes. "Boy, I wouldn't want to be in your shoes as far as Jemimah is concerned," she said.

Romero sighed. "I'm pretty sure she's already come to

terms with the situation, at least I hope so. So, when did you start working on Sundays?"

"Just came by to pick up a couple of files. I'll be working at the main office this week," Clarissa said.

"You can table that for now. It looks like I'll be in town for the duration. No need for you to hang around here any longer, so go home." He headed for his office and dialed Jemimah's cell. She picked up on the first ring.

"For a minute there I thought you'd gone off on our honeymoon without me," she laughed.

"Not hardly," he said. "Just another damned murder out in the hills. Poor guy, hopefully we can get an ID on him soon and get his family notified. I'll probably know a little more by morning. I should be home in a few."

"We'll have to figure out something for dinner. I had already emptied out the fridge in anticipation of being gone for a while," she said.

"Let me just order a pizza. I could use a cold beer right about now." He waved to Clarissa on his way out. The pizza place was five minutes from the substation and his order was ready when he pulled into the drive-up. He retrieved his change and drove around the corner to the general store to pick up a six pack of Corona.

At home, the couple stretched out on the couch, a half-empty pizza carton on the coffee table. Jemimah's dog, Molly, sat on the nearby hassock, eyeing the leftovers, while out in the yard, Gato the cat mewed soulfully at the barn door, hoping to continue the chase for the mouse that had been eluding him all afternoon. They were the only ones happy about the honeymoon delay. Jemimah had picked Molly up from the dog-sitter early that afternoon.

"I know you probably don't want to talk shop, but tell me a little about this case," Jemimah said.

"Dammit, I had hoped we wouldn't be talking shop for a couple of weeks, but here we are," Romero said.

Jemimah smoothed the side of his head. "Did you actually

believe that as a cop you could have any kind of normal life, honeymoons included?"

"One could hope, but truthfully, I doubt it. I'm sorry, Jem, this really sucks."

"Yes, murder usually does, and life sometimes takes a dip in the road. So, is the victim local?"

"I don't think so, but there wasn't any ID on him. We'll know more when the guys finish canvassing the scene. I'm pretty sure the dispatch I received about an abandoned Ford a couple of miles away from the area might give us a better idea," he said.

"You think it might be connected?"

"Looks like it. Too coincidental to have an abandoned vehicle so close to a crime scene. Hard to say what this is going to develop into. To begin with, a crime in the woods is always difficult to solve. Forensic evidence is usually scattered by shifting winds and foraging animals. Doesn't take long for the entire scene to be eroded to some degree. However, it appears he hadn't been dead too long. We'll see what the coroner has to say."

Romero yawned and stretched out his arm to cradle her shoulders. "I know one thing for sure, Sweetie. We don't need a sandy beach to get that honeymoon started." He laughed and reached for her hand and pulled her to her feet.

She smiled. "That's an invitation I can't refuse."

Chapter Six

———❖———

FOR MORE THAN three years, Jemimah Hodge had been employed by the Santa Fe County Sheriff's Office as a Forensic Psychologist. She had worked alongside Lieutenant Detective Romero and his staff to interview witnesses and suspects, and in several cases had been instrumental in solving major crimes. It was at this job where they met. Initially, their relationship had taken a few wrong turns. She just didn't like him as much as it appeared he liked her. And then, somewhere along the way, between murder investigations and witness interviews, they fell in love.

Jemimah had never entirely given up her belief in God, but it was no longer the Mormon god, it was the universal God. She felt at home sitting in a pew at the Cathedral in downtown Santa Fe, or lighting a candle at the home altar Romero maintained for his mother. There was no doubt they wanted a priest to officiate their wedding.

Once they decided to get married, they knew this step would require a reality check on both their parts. They both had long been aware that County regulations did not allow husbands and wives to work together, especially in law enforcement. More than likely, it would be necessary for one of them to relinquish their job. Jemimah knew she couldn't ask Rick to give up his long career as head detective for the Sheriff's Department. Although she hated to give up her own position, it appeared that was the only solution, so she resigned a week before the wedding date.

She had spent most of that Monday pondering what her options were. She could dust off her shingle and resume her practice as a licensed psychologist. She also thought about becoming a private detective and opening her own office, but after she checked into the prospects, she decided against that. It would involve working a lot harder than she ever did for the County, and probably couldn't turn it off at five o'clock and go home. She would also miss the time they could spend together. They were in the early stages of adjusting to married life, and that additional stress wouldn't help.

It wasn't as though Jemimah needed a job right away, but she wanted one. She wasn't someone who could be idle for long periods of time. She decided she would spend a week or so spring-cleaning the house and barn and then make her decision while replanning the eventual honeymoon trip. She had hired a neighboring teen to muck out the stalls, lay down fresh straw, clean the water troughs, put out feed and shovel manure from the paddocks. Once that was done she would focus on the house. In a discussion the previous night, Rick asked why she didn't take a few months off. After all, she hadn't had a real vacation for as long as he'd known her, with the exception of a few weekend trips they took together.

"Our honeymoon was going to be my vacation," she had said.

"Well, there's no reason why you can't just extend the time off for a couple of months and get yourself well rested," he said. Darling that he was, he then asked why she needed to work at all.

"Are you kidding me? What would I do, stay at home and watch reality TV all day, munching on chips and salsa?"

He laughed. "That's not what I meant. You could invest in

some high-end camera equipment and start photographing every place you ever wanted to visit. The photos you took of the Bisti Badlands on our trip last fall were good enough for a cover on the New Mexico Magazine. You could also teach a couple of courses at UNM, and start on that book you've been talking about."

Jemimah tilted her head. "I guess I'm just not cut out for the sedentary lifestyle, Rick. I've been on my own for so long, it's hard to sit still. And, besides, camera equipment is really expensive."

He put his hand on her arm. "If it's help you need, Sweetie, I've saved up a small chunk of cash over the years."

"That's very sweet, and I appreciate the offer, but I think I'll hit the pavement in a few days and find myself another exciting job. Who knows, there may be something sitting out there in plain sight."

He frowned. "Damn, I'm sorry we were forced to make the decision about which one of us was going to give up our position with the County. I know how you loved your job."

"In a way, I'm unhappy about that too, but I'm not sorry I married you. Rules are rules, and we knew it going in. It's unlikely that the County will make an exception in our case. Sheriff Medrano turned a blind eye to our relationship longer than he should have, and he tried like hell to get the commissioners to make some changes in the rules. Bottom line, I'm sure going to miss working side by side with you."

"As am I," Romero said, touching her cheek.

Jemimah realized she had been mulling over the previous night's conversation with Rick longer than she had intended. She tidied up the kitchen and headed into the bedroom to get dressed for the day.

Chapter Seven

------◆------

JEMIMAH'S CELL PHONE rang as she exited the shower. Wrapped in a towel, she saw that it was Sheriff Medrano. *I wonder what he wants. Probably calling to apologize for screwing up our honeymoon.*

Indeed, he did apologize, and then asked her to drop by the office to take care of some paperwork. Jemimah agreed to stop there shortly before noon. She walked over to her closet and picked out something to wear. She opted for black slacks and a long-sleeved pink Henley top. A dusting of blush, mascara and lipstick, and she was out the door.

As she drove down Highway 14 toward the County complex at Exit 599, a list of options trickled through her mind. Once she signed her release papers, she would definitely be on her own. Oh, well, she wasn't going to think about it. She had always managed to land on her feet, and she had a feeling this wasn't going to be any different. She figured a brisk walk would help clear her head and she steered her vehicle into a parking spot several blocks from the entrance to the County compound. Inside the main entrance, the guard ran her handbag through the security check, and signed her in. Along her way down the hall to Sheriff Medrano's office, she was greeted by a number of employees, including deputies she had worked with in the past. Medrano's secretary waved Jemimah in and showed her to the back office.

The Sheriff stood to meet her, directing her to the chair next to his desk. "Jemimah, how nice to see you again. My wife and I both thought the wedding was beautiful."

Jemimah smiled. "Yes, it was. Thank you."

He lowered himself into the chair. "I don't have to tell you again how sorry I am that we had to pull Rick away at the last minute. Couldn't be helped. You know how that is," he said.

"Yes, I understand. I never doubted for a moment that it couldn't be avoided." Jemimah shifted in her seat. "So, tell me, Eddie, what documents to do you need me to sign to take care of my termination? And while we're at it, I would also like to put in for my accumulated time off, if that's not a problem."

Medrano shuffled the papers on his desk and handed her a file folder. "Take a look through these and tell me what you think," he said.

Jemimah methodically skimmed through the pages. A puzzled look crossed her face. She looked up to see Medrano with a big grin on his face.

"I don't understand," she said.

"Let me explain, Doctor Hodge. While you two were finalizing your wedding plans, I had a couple of meetings last week with the County supervisors. It turns out that they decided to modify a few of the requirements regarding nepotism and related matters. Consequently, it appeared that prohibiting married couples from working together in law enforcement was depriving them of their rights to employment," he said. "Not wanting to get in trouble with the Feds, they eased up on the rules. Therefore, I'm offering you a position in the newly established Forensic Science Department. You will continue to be the Chief Forensic Psychologist and it also means a well-deserved bump in pay. What do you think?"

Jemimah was in shock. "I don't know what to say, Sheriff. I came here expecting to sign my formal resignation. Yes, of course, I accept." She came around his desk and hugged him.

"I thought you might accept," he smiled. "And you and Rick are still going to have that honeymoon in Mexico. Might be a short while before it happens, but it will, just as soon as some of the detectives complete their FBI course requirements and return to duty." He made a shooshing motion with his hands. "Now get out of here and go tell that husband of yours the good news so I can get some work done."

She pushed her seat back and stood. "I don't know how to thank you, Eddie," she said.

"No thanks necessary. You've been a star in our department for a couple of years, and it's time all that hard work was recognized."

Chapter Eight

THAT MONDAY MORNING, Detective Romero met Tim McCabe at the San Marcos Café & Feedstore just north of the Village of Cerrillos on the alternate highway between Santa Fe and Albuquerque. The café was a favored spot for both Sheriff's deputies and State Policemen, along with locals who frequented the small establishment well known for its chile-laden breakfasts. Outside there was an old buckboard wagon filled with firewood left over from the previous winter. Noisy peacocks strutted around the yard, their tail feathers fanned out with iridescent blues and greens. The interior was homey, with wood sideboards, cabinets, tables and chairs placed around the seating area. An old iron wood stove stood in the corner next to shelves filled with historical knickknacks.

Tim McCabe had been Romero's friend and associate deputy for several years. He was a retired lawman from Idaho who served in an advisory capacity to the Cerrillos substation. He was owner of the only private Indian ruins in Northern New Mexico, along with a many-acred ranch adjoining the ruins. He and his wife, Laura, split their time between the ranch and their Canyon Road home in Santa Fe. Over the years the couple had amassed a large collection of Native American and Spanish Colonial art which they sold at auction when they sold the gallery the previous year.

During that time, McCabe became a well-known celebrity for having buried a treasure valued at over a million dollars somewhere in the southwest. He was a popular guest of major network morning shows, where each Tuesday of the month he revealed a new clue to its whereabouts. So far there had been thousands of searchers, but as of yet, not one lucky person had claimed the elusive wooden chest.

They made their way through the main room and sat at a corner table with ladder-back chairs. The waitress upended the china cups and filled them with steaming coffee, setting a pitcher of cream next to them. After their order was placed, Romero filled McCabe in on the latest developments.

He wasn't surprised to hear that a body had been discovered near his property. It had only been a little over a year that the body of a popular Mariachi was found not too far from this one. The out of the way area served as a prime location for beer busts and target practice.

McCabe thoughtfully stirred cream into his coffee. "Don't know what it is about the area. Hundreds of years ago, the entire acreage was populated by several Pueblo Indian tribes, most of whom scattered after the 1680 Pueblo Revolt," he said, between bites of his breakfast burrito.

"Could be some kind of curse," Romero offered.

McCabe nodded. "I sure took care of that on the Indian ruins abutting the ranch property. I had a group of tribal elders conduct a healing ceremony. Guess that smudging and drumming didn't extend out far enough."

"Hard to say," Romero said. "There's always something spooky going on around here. Even at the substation, Clarissa tells me she hears doors slamming and flute music playing at random times. Guess I'm going to have to hire a shaman to come and sage the place."

McCabe laughed. "That or move the offices down the road somewhere."

"Yeah, sure. As if the County would allow that. They like us just where we are. The arm of the law protecting the smaller villages." Romero's phone buzzed. He looked down at the screen. On the line was the dispatcher with news regarding the abandoned rental car.

"Excuse me, Tim. Gotta take this."

"Detective, the records from the Hertz rental office at the airport in Albuquerque indicate that the car was rented to a Lawrence Tanner from Provo, Utah. It was supposed to be returned a few days ago. I'll email you whatever information I can get from them."

"Thanks, Dorothy. We'll take care of it from here. McCabe and I will drive over and take a look at it." He turned to McCabe. "If you're not doing anything after breakfast, do you mind riding out to the crime scene with me? That rental car might be the one the victim was driving. I'll get the crime techs to meet us out there."

On the way to the site Romero's phone beeped. The dispatcher sent a copy of the document allowing the Sheriff's office to impound the vehicle for their investigation, along with a copy of the driver's license on record. He passed the phone to McCabe, who took a look at the documents.

"I prefer the old way of solving cases before social media ruled the universe. Emailing, texting, twittering...what else is coming down the pike," he said.

Romero chuckled. "That's *tweeting*. And you forgot Instagram and Facebook and a few other social sites. But bear in mind that in an investigation, law enforcement has access to pretty much all of it, and sometimes it turns out to be helpful."

McCabe handed the phone back to Romero. "Sure, if there's sufficient cause for a judge to sign a warrant. Otherwise, it's all off limits."

"Well, no matter how long it takes, the stuff can't be erased. You can destroy a cell phone or a computer, but the good thing is that the information still resides with the server. Didn't have that in the old days. In recent years, many cases have been solved by law enforcement being able to access critical texts and emails sent or received by a victim."

"Yeah, I hear you. I guess some of us are still stuck in the eighties," he said.

"Hopefully info from dispatch will help us find out a little more about the victim and allow us to notify the next of kin. He's been sitting in the morgue since Sunday, and our investigation has been hampered by our inability to identify him," Romero said. As he turned onto the dirt road, he could see the crime tech van up ahead.

The interior of the vehicle was dusted for fingerprints. Under the front seat, the detective found a wallet and cell phone. He reached for them with a gloved hand. In the wallet was a driver's license identical to the copy forwarded from the rental company, along with a credit card receipt from a motel on Cerrillos Road, and eighty dollars in cash.

The victim was indeed Lawrence Tanner, who resided at an address in Provo, Utah. There was also a stack of business cards indicating the victim was affiliated in some manner with the Mormon Church. Romero photographed the items, marked them as evidence and then placed all the information in a Ziploc bag and handed them to the tech, who placed them in larger bag. When Romero returned to his office, he would make a few phone calls, send a copy of the driver's license to the coroner's office and have them compare it to the body.

McCabe stood by as the trunk to the vehicle was opened. Inside was a small Coleman stove, a case of water, and a few miscellaneous camping items, along with an extra pair of hiking shoes.

"This wasn't a burglary. Our perp could have retrieved the victim's keys and come back and emptied the trunk and the wallet. In fact, he could have run off with the backpack itself. Looks like our victim was going to do a little camping. Not exactly the best place for it, but to each his own," said McCabe.

"First-time camper, I imagine." Romero said as he checked his notes. "The victim was covered with a sleeping bag. Why would that be the only camping item he had with him and everything else was in the car?"

McCabe scratched his head. "Maybe he was getting ready to camp out and hadn't transported everything to the site yet."

"Sounds reasonable, but the car was parked quite a distance away. We'll have to figure that one out," said Romero.

They took another quick look around, talked to the tech for a few minutes, and then took off. Romero dropped McCabe off at the restaurant to retrieve his vehicle.

"I'm going to be making a few phone calls. That's the part of my job that I hate the most, trying to locate and notify the next of kin," Romero said.

"I don't envy you that job," McCabe said.

Fifteen minutes later he sat at his desk, having printed out photos he had taken of the contents of the victim's wallet. He called the number on one of the cards and waited while the recording played through. He punched the number eight to talk to the bishop. That sounded like it would be a good place to start. A man with a gravelly voice answered and identified himself as Bishop Kimball.

Romero introduced himself and explained to the bishop what the purpose of the call was.

"I'm sorry to report that the Santa Fe County Sheriff's Office is in the middle of an investigation," he said.

"Where did you say you were calling from?"

"Santa Fe, New Mexico. I'm calling about a gentleman named Lawrence Tanner. Is that name familiar to you?"

There was a pause. "Yes, of course, Lawrence Tanner. What is this about? Mr. Tanner is a member of our church, and is studying toward becoming a bishop. Is something wrong, has there been an accident?"

"First I need some information. Can you tell me what he was doing in New Mexico?" Romero said.

"He was there to speak to a group of members from the Mormon Church in Albuquerque. Then I understand he was going to take a few days to take in the sights of Santa Fe. He was supposed to be back sometime soon, if I'm not mistaken. Now, may I ask again what this is about, Detective?" the bishop said.

"I'm sorry to inform you that Mr. Tanner has been the victim of what appears to be a homicide. I'm looking to notify the next of kin," Romero said.

Another pause. "Homicide...My God, what happened?" he said.

"I'm not at liberty to divulge the details, sir. The crime is still under investigation. Positive identification was made from a Utah driver's license found in his wallet along with his Social Security Card and a number of credit cards. Do you know if Mr. Tanner had a family?"

"No, I believe he was divorced a few years back. No children. He does have a fiancée, though. That would be a Miss Eliza Simpson. Oh, my, this is terrible news. She's going to be devastated," he said. "They were planning on being married this summer."

"I'd like to ask her a few questions, if you don't mind giving her my number. I'll be here for another hour or so," Romero said. He thanked Bishop Kimball, punched the off button and then dialed Jemimah's cell.

"Well, Detective, I was wondering when you'd get around to calling. Are you able to have lunch? I have some news," she said.

"Sure, let's do that," he said. "Swing by the office and pick me up, and then we'll decide where."

Before he could grab his keys and walk out to the parking lot to meet Jemimah, the phone rang. Caller ID reflected the same area code as the call he made earlier regarding the victim. He punched the talk button and could hear a woman sobbing in the background. Dealing with grief-stricken relatives was still the most uncomfortable part of the detective's job.

"Detective Romero, here," he answered.

"I'm sorry, Detective. My name is Eliza Simpson. I'm calling from Provo, Utah. Our bishop just called me to say

Lawrence Tanner had been found dead," she said. "There has to be a mistake, how can this be?"

"What is your relationship to Mr. Tanner, if I might ask?"

She paused. "I am..was..his fiancée."

Romero could tell she was struggling to maintain her composure. "I'm so sorry for your loss, Miss Simpson. We have confirmed the identity of Mr. Tanner. Do you feel up to answering a few questions?"

She broke into sobs and after a long pause, she returned to the call. "Detective, can I get in touch with you later today? I thought I could do this, but I just can't seem to stop crying. This is such a shock."

"Of course, I understand. Take your time. You have my contact information." He stared at the phone after she hung up, feeling sorry for the woman at the other end of the line. It appeared to him that her nightmare had just begun.

Chapter Nine

JEMIMAH SAT IN her 4Runner, clipped on the seat belt, checked the mirror and applied a dab of color to her lips. She started up the engine and drove out onto the highway toward the substation and Romero's office. Because of her meeting with Sheriff Medrano earlier in the day, she was filled with excitement and couldn't wait to tell Rick the news. She had thought of calling him, but decided she wanted to witness his reaction in person. She knew he would be as thrilled as she was.

The two met some years before when Jemimah was riding her horse on the Indian ruins next to the Crawford ranch and found Tim McCabe on the ground, having been shot in the chest. The case exploded when Jemimah and McCabe discovered the bodies of five missing women in a tunnel beneath the Indian ruins, a case that would join Romero in the investigation. That encounter was the impetus that propelled Jemimah into her current job, first as a profiler and then as a forensic psychologist. Since the couple met, they had been adversaries, friends, and then lovers, with a few fallings out in between, and now husband and wife. She was ecstatic that they would still be working together on cases. She was looking forward to the challenges presented by a homicide where she could pore over the evidence and form a profile of the suspects.

The blare of the horn from an eighteen-wheeler startled her. Due to ongoing construction, the road had narrowed and the trucker was traveling too fast to slow down to forty-five and he wanted her out of the way. Jemimah's hands clenched the steering wheel as the driver laid on the horn and she pulled over to the side to give him room. That driving infraction carried a huge fine. She reached for her notebook and jotted down the mile marker and the 800 number on the back of the vehicle, which read, *Am I driving safely?* She wondered, where were the cops when you needed them, and chuckled at the irony as she took the turn into the driveway where Romero was leaning against his vehicle, waiting.

He opened the passenger door and leaned over to kiss her. "Your cheeks are flushed. Are you that happy to see me?"

She returned the kiss and grinned. "You betcha. I have some great news, but it can wait until we get to the restaurant. I'm starving."

"The closest place is *El Parasol*, then. I'm up for a couple of tamales and a side of red."

The drive to the restaurant took less than ten minutes. Jemimah told him about her experience with the trucker as she parked next to a bus filled with tourists. They hurried into the restaurant to get ahead of the crowd. *El Parasol*, which translated to *the umbrella*, was a small restaurant at the 599 exit from Highway 14. A colorful beach umbrella was their logo, and they specialized in well prepared quick Mexican food. It was a popular venue for travelers and employees of nearby businesses. Jemimah laughed about how odd it was to have a beach umbrella sticking out into the desert sky on a road called Dinosaur Drive. Only in New Mexico.

Seated at a table on the covered patio, the couple placed their order and the waitress brought two glasses of iced tea to the table. Romero reached across for Jemimah's hand.

"Okay, now what's this good news you've been bubbling

over with for the last half hour? Did you decide to go out and buy yourself a camera?"

Jemimah couldn't wait to blurt out her news. She told him about her meeting with Medrano, having fully expected him to shake her hand and thank her for her good work and then send her on her way. But that it had turned out much different than she ever expected, and she was still going to be employed by the County. "You are looking at the head of the new Forensic Sciences Department," she said.

He scooted closer and embraced her. "Jem, that's the best news I've heard in a long time! I was feeling so guilty about you having to give up your job."

"I'm excited, too. I start back on Monday. That's just a few days away, so I need to hit the grocery store and stock up the refrigerator. From the looks of your current case load, it appears as though our honeymoon is still up in the air?"

"Yes, it is, but I'm hopeful it will happen soon. This new case isn't moving very fast, but we're on it. Just getting the preliminaries out of the way." He brought her up to date, including that the victim had just been identified and he was in the process of getting some information from the man's fiancée, who had called as he was leaving the office.

"Poor thing. I imagine she's pretty devastated, particularly having to hear the news by phone," Jemimah said.

Romero spooned up the last of his meal and pushed the plate aside, patting his stomach. "Yeah, she was. Couldn't hardly talk. Said she'd call me back in a few hours. I need to catch up on some paperwork, so when we're done here, if you drop me back at the office," he said. "I'll keep you in the loop on this one. There's bound to be some witnesses coming out of the woodwork soon."

Jemimah marveled at how things can change in a moment's time. When she woke up this morning she was unemployed and hopeful about the prospects in finding a job. Now, without skipping a beat, she was looking forward to working on a homicide. She chided herself for that last thought.

Chapter Ten

———·———

Late that Monday afternoon, Eliza Simpson slowly tapped the detective's number into her phone. She was barely over the shock of the news she had received earlier, but knew she had to return his call.

"Detective Romero, this is Eliza Simpson again," she said, "Lawrence Tanner's fiancée. Is this a good time?"

"Yes, Miss Simpson. Thank you for getting back to me. Are you sure you're up to answering a few questions?"

"I am, and I know it's important to get this over with. So, tell me, what is it you want to know," she said.

"These are fairly standard questions, Ma'am, so whatever additional information you can offer that might be of some help. Do you know if the victim, Mr. Tanner, had any connections to New Mexico other than his recent visit here?"

"I don't believe so. He was just there to meet with Mormon Church officials and discuss future meetings regarding our young missionaries," she said. "I don't think he'd ever visited there before."

Romero scribbled in his notebook. "How long have you known him?"

"About two years. We were both divorced and single, and

started dating sometime after that." She paused. "We had just become engaged."

"This might sound harsh, but are you aware of any individual who might have had it in for him?"

"What do you mean?"

"Anyone who disliked or hated him, any previous confrontations he might have had? Anyone seeking to harm him?"

She responded quickly. "Oh, no. Lawrence was a good man. He was kind and thoughtful. I never heard him have a harsh word with anyone. Everyone thought very highly of him. He was studying to eventually become a bishop in the Mormon Church, but first he had to overcome a few obstacles."

"And what might those obstacles be?" Romero asked.

"Oh, they relate to church doctrine. I'm sure you don't want to hear an explanation of that," she said.

"Go ahead," he said. "It might be helpful."

She inhaled deeply. "Well, in the Mormon Church, divorce is not technically a divorce like most people are used to. It is more of a temple sealing cancellation, which means that the prior marriage is annulled. It can take anywhere from a few months to a year or longer."

"Had there been any problems with that process?"

"Oh, no. The necessity for an annulment doesn't arise until either of the divorced couple is seeking to be sealed to a new wife, which in our case would be coming up before we could be married. Does that make sense to you, Detective?" she said.

"I can see where it wouldn't enter into my investigation. Doesn't seem to involve anything surreptitious," he said.

She was silent for a moment. "On another subject, Detective, could I ask what the process is for returning the body back to Utah for burial? Lawrence didn't have any close relatives, so it will be up to the church to make funeral arrangements."

Romero put her on speaker phone and pushed his chair closer to the desk. "There is a process that has to be followed. Once the autopsy has been completed, then the body will be released. It will probably take about a week for that to happen," he said.

"Autopsy?" she said. "Why is that necessary?"

Romero preferred to not to discuss the cause of death with her. "Standard procedure, Ma'am. The coroner examines the body and determines the cause of death and then issues the death certificate. After that the body is released."

She was silent. "Thank you. Do you have any other questions?"

"I believe that's it. You've been of some help. If you don't mind, I might contact you in the future if I need additional information. Again, I'm sorry for your loss, Miss Simpson."

She thanked him and hung up the phone. Romero scribbled a list on the tablet and then closed his notebook turned off the lights in the building, locked up, and headed out to his cruiser.

Chapter Eleven

JEMIMAH'S RANCHETTE WAS a nice-sized bungalow with wide porches in front and back. The rear of the house overlooked the Ortiz Mountains and the front faced the Garden of the Gods, a city-sized block of ancient monolithic stone formations running along Highway 14, which was also known as the Turquoise Trail. The whole area was historic, having been part of the aftermath of the 1680 Pueblo Revolt, where thousands of Spaniards and Indians lost their lives in battle.

On the other side of Santa Fe, Romero had inherited his family home on a shady side street in the South Capitol area, a 1940s two-bedroom adobe in the heart of the city. Although desirable, the area was nowhere near the demand of the high-end condos and multi-million dollar homes a few blocks away in the affluent east side neighborhoods of East Garcia Street and Camino del Monte Sol. When the couple became engaged, they decided it would be easier for them to live at Jemimah's residence because of the animals and spend one night a week at the Santa Fe house.

The month had passed the halfway mark, the days slipping by like pages of a good mystery. Jemimah had stocked the fridge and Romero had propped himself at the kitchen counter with an array of grocery items set out before him. In a bowl were avocados, tomatoes, cheese, onions and a lemon, along with an assortment of hot peppers, all of which he intended to finely chop and dice to make a batch of chile rellenos with a side of guacamole. He reached for the metal tongs and pulled the roasted green chile peppers from the broiler and placed them in a wooden bowl covered with a damp tea towel so they could sweat and facilitate peeling. The aroma filled the kitchen as he carefully removed the stems. When he peeled the last one in the bowl, he set them aside while he thinly sliced a half moon of longhorn cheese.

He heard Molly barking out in the front yard. It wasn't her aggressive bark, but the special one filled with dog joy reserved for Jemimah as the two returned from an hour's walk in the nearby hills. The Border Collie enjoyed the open landscape around the ranch, and at seven years old, was starting to show her age. When at the Santa Fe house, she would curl up in front of the fireplace or snuggle between the couple and snooze while they watched TV, but out in the country she still enjoyed chasing jackrabbits.

The two bounded through the back door. Molly headed for the water bowl and Jemimah to the sink to wash her hands. She had spent most of the day catching up on household chores and grocery shopping. Ever since Rick had moved in, the place seemed smaller. Nice thing about it, though, he picked up after himself quite nicely and did his own laundry. She smiled. All those years as a bachelor were paying off. Since their engagement, they had experienced a deeper love and companionship than ever before. She hoped their working together again would not interfere with the magic of their relationship.

She took two glasses from the cupboard, uncorked a bottle of wine and poured him a full glass. "You seem a little quiet there. Long day?"

"Pretty much. After you dropped me off I had another

conversation with the fiancée of the victim. No telling how this case is going to turn out. Once we get the autopsy and the report from the crime techs, maybe it will start moving forward." He turned to face her. "Meanwhile, my sweet thing, gonna have to mute the work channel and enjoy a home-cooked meal together."

She laughed. "That would be nice. I need to stop eating out, otherwise I'm going to have to sign up at the gym."

He patted her behind. "You're perfect just as you are. I don't know anyone who gets more exercise than you do. Between the dog and the horse, I think that's plenty enough."

They carried their trays into the living room, where Molly was already laid out on the loveseat, snuggled into the sheepskin rug. She looked at them with one eye open and then rolled on her back and fell asleep as the hungry couple dug into their dinner.

Chapter Twelve

————◆————

THE QUIET OF the evening was interrupted by Romero's cell phone connected to the charger in the bedroom. He reached across the bed to answer it. On the other end was the Mormon bishop to whom he had spoken earlier.

"Detective," he said. "This is Bishop Kimball. I hope I'm not interrupting your dinner. I just realized we're an hour earlier here than you are."

"Not at all," Romero said. "What can I do for you?"

"Well," he said. "After we hung up and I relayed the bad news to his fiancée, I had a few thoughts about a matter I counseled Lawrence about over a year ago. Do you have a minute?"

Romero reached for a pen and notebook and returned to the living room. He sat next to Jemimah. "Yes, of course, go on."

"I have to go back and review the session in detail, but as I recall it had something to do with an FLDS leader who was moving his group to somewhere in New Mexico and apparently had an involvement with Lawrence's ex-wife," he said.

"FLDS? What is that?" Romero noticed Jemimah glance at him with a question on her face.

"The FLDS, Fundamentalist Church of Jesus Christ of Latter Day Saints, is a radical offshoot of mainstream Mormonism."

"What makes them different from Mormons?"

"Oh, there is a vast difference," the Bishop said. "The Mormon Church disavowed polygamy more than a hundred years ago. These radical groups have developed their own lifestyle of living, many involving multiple wives and scores of children," he said.

"Can you tell me what Tanner's involvement was with this group?"

"It wasn't a personal involvement, per se," he said. "It was some sort of dispute he had with one of the members of the movement."

"Can you give me any of the specifics?" Romero said.

He hesitated. "I apologize, but I'm going to have to review my files in detail, which unfortunately are locked up in the church offices. I won't have access to them until morning, but I certainly will make it a point to contact you then," he said. "I hate to appear so vague, but I wanted to mention this before it slipped my mind," the Bishop said. "If I don't write things down, I tend to forget."

"Thank you, Bishop Kimball. I look forward to any additional information you can provide." Romero ended the call and set his phone on the lamp table. Jemimah was staring at him.

"What was that about?" she said.

"This is interesting. Are you aware of any FLDS groups settling here in New Mexico?"

Jemimah nodded. "Vaguely. I read something about a year ago regarding a group that started up in the southern area of the state after Warren Jeffs was imprisoned. I understand they tried to bilk the state out of thousands of dollars in welfare benefits. Don't remember hearing anything more after that. It's pretty unlikely any group would move into the state after receiving so much adverse publicity."

As the couple retired to the bedroom, Jemimah recalled

that her father had been an active member of the FLDS. Her stomach tightened at the memory. She took a deep breath and set the thought aside.

Chapter Thirteen

F OLLOWING A FRIDAY morning meeting with Sheriff
Medrano, Detective Romero was headed to the substation
when his cell phone rang. He glanced down to see Clarissa's
name on the screen, and picked it up.

"Where are you, Boss?" she asked.

"Just walked out of my meeting with Medrano. Stopped by
to pick up some coffee and donuts and heading in. Should be
there in a few. What's up?"

"There's a woman here waiting to see you. She says she
doesn't have an appointment, but that you'll know who she is.
I have her in the waiting room," Clarissa said.

"Who is it?"

"She says her name is Eliza Simpson and she spoke to you
on the phone last Friday. I told her I wasn't sure when you'd
be available, but she said she needed to see you," Clarissa said.

Romero looked at his watch. "Have her wait. I'm on my
way." He pulled out his earpiece and slipped the phone in his
pocket. He wondered why the woman would be so insistent on
waiting for him, but he would know soon enough.

He drove into the substation lot and parked in his reserved
space on the side of the building. He carried his briefcase, the

coffee and donuts up the walk. Clarissa met him at the door, relieved him of the box and nodded her head toward the woman sitting on the couch in the waiting room with her head bowed and her hands in her lap.

Eliza Simpson was an attractive woman, dressed fashionably in a matching beige shirt jacket and trousers. Her short brown hair was curly and framed an oval face with dark brown eyes. She didn't appear as distraught as she had over the phone. Romero told Clarissa to give him a minute and then bring her into his office.

"Miss Simpson. Come in and have a seat. I wasn't expecting to see you. Is there something in particular you need to discuss? I assume you're in Santa Fe about making arrangements?" he said.

She nodded as she pulled up a chair in front of Romero's desk.

"I believe I mentioned that the arrangements could not be made until the autopsy was conducted." Romero thumbed through his Daybook. "That's scheduled early next week. Once the coroner releases the body, then you can get in touch with the funeral home to make arrangements."

She nodded again. "Yes, I understand. I apologize for not contacting you in advance, but after we talked on the phone, I met with the bishop and he told me about your conversation with him. I decided I might as well come here and speak to you in person. I might have something to add to the information the bishop gave you, now that my head is a little clearer."

Romero stood. "Before we continue, can I offer you a cup of coffee or water?"

She shook her head, the curls springing with the movement. "I'm fine, thank you."

"In order to put a face to the name, I'd like for you to take a look at Mr. Tanner's driver's license and identify him. If you feel you need to see him, I can also arrange that."

Eliza Simpson turned her face to the side. "No, no. I don't want to do that." She looked at the license and handed it back to Romero. "Yes, that's him."

Romero pulled out a yellow pad and made note of her information. "All right. What is it you wanted to discuss with me?"

Eliza Simpson crossed her legs and leaned forward in her seat. "Well, after our initial conversation, my mind was a complete blank, as you can well understand. The news I received was shocking, to say the least. Over the weekend I remembered something Lawrence said a while back." She paused to take a breath.

"What was that?" Romero said.

"Well, you asked about any connection he might have had to New Mexico, and since I'm not too familiar with the state, I couldn't picture it in my head. I haven't traveled the southwest as much as I'd like to.

"I don't know if this is relevant, but the bishop might have mentioned that Lawrence had been divorced?"

"Yes, I believe he did."

"I recall Lawrence mentioned that after he and his wife broke up, it wasn't too long before she took up with a fellow who had several wives. Maybe she was even seeing him during the marriage, he didn't know for sure."

"A polygamist?" Romero said.

"Yes, and that this man was encouraging her to move to New Mexico with him and become part of his group."

"As a member?" Romero asked.

"No, I believe he wanted her to become his next wife," she said.

"What was your fiancé's reaction to that?" Romero said.

She smoothed the front of her trousers, straightening the seam. "Personally, I think it bothered him a little, since they had been together for quite a few years, but his only remark was that she was an adult and could do whatever she pleased."

Romero scribbled a note on the pad. "Do you know what name the ex-wife goes by?"

"Yes, Brigid. Brigid Tanner."

"How do you spell that?" he said.

"B-r-i-g-i-d. I don't think she changed back to her maiden name, and I don't know what that was." She dropped her hands to her lap. "That's pretty much all I can remember. The subject never came up again, and I didn't feel the need to pursue it."

Romero inquired where she would be staying and how long she planned to be in Santa Fe. "There might be other questions that come up as we get further into our investigation. At the appropriate time, I'll have someone from our Forensic Science Department contact you about preparing what we refer to as a witness interview statement, so we can get all this into the record."

He stood and thanked her, then buzzed Clarissa to show her out. He picked up the phone and speed dialed Tim McCabe. Not only was McCabe his best buddy, but over the years he had become Romero's right-hand man. The detective could always depend on the more experienced lawman to add needed insight to a case.

Chapter Fourteen

Tim and Laura McCabe had been married for over forty years. They met in Ruidoso, New Mexico, where her father raised thoroughbred racing horses and McCabe hired on from Idaho to troubleshoot some security issues the company was experiencing. The couple had an immediate connection and when McCabe returned to his job as sheriff of a small town in Idaho, he couldn't get Laura out of his mind. He traveled back to New Mexico, and after a considerable time, convinced her to marry him. They settled first in Idaho and then moved to Santa Fe, where for years they operated a high-end gallery on Canyon road which specialized in Western and Spanish Colonial artifacts. Twenty years later, they sold the gallery and the contents and split their time between the Canyon Road house and the recently remodeled ranch which adjoined the San Lazaro Pueblo Indian ruins in Cerrillos.

Two years earlier, McCabe and his partner, Foster Burke, joined in a venture which made national headlines. After much planning, they offered out a hidden treasure to the public, an antique wooden chest filled with items consisting of over a million dollars' worth of gems, coins and artifacts. Eventually, Foster pulled back and moved to his casita in Cabo

San Lucas, Mexico, leaving the more gregarious McCabe to field the publicity and interviews resulting from the initial announcement and the promotion of McCabe's book, which was riddled with clues to the location of the treasure. Tens of thousands of emails and inquiries later, the treasure had still not been found. McCabe had become a national celebrity, appearing regularly on major news shows to talk about the antique chest and its contents.

The couple had just finished a late breakfast in the portal of their home when the phone rang. Laura picked up on the third ring, smiled and handed Tim the phone.

"It's your other boss."

McCabe returned the smile and kissed her hand as he took the phone.

"Tim, I need your help to do a little checking around," Romero said.

"Sure, what's going on?"

"I need you to check if in the past year or so there's been any activity involving a polygamist sect moving into New Mexico," Romero said, "particularly around the northern half of the state."

"You mean the guys with multiple wives?"

"Exactly. You familiar with them?"

"Oh, sure," McCabe said. "When we lived in Idaho, every so often a group of polygamists would settle in around the fringes, but most of the time the weather and terrain proved to be a little harsh and they moved on. I think there are currently a few settlements in the southern part of Colorado, if I'm not mistaken," McCabe said.

"You know more about it than I do, then. I'd appreciate you looking into this. Let me know what you find out," Romero said.

"Will do," McCabe said, ending the call.

Laura waved a finger at him. "I take it that means you won't be helping me dig up the bulbs in the garden," she said.

Tim started to say something. Laura gently pushed on

his shoulder with her fingers. "Go on. I can get Rosa to help. Unlike some people, she enjoys working in the garden," she chuckled.

He kissed her on the cheek. "Thank you, my dear. I knew you'd understand." He went down the hall to the bedroom to retrieve his wallet and keychain. Out in the garage, he backed the Hummer out onto the circular drive and waved to Laura as he drove out onto the street. It was a ten minute drive to downtown Santa Fe and he scored a parking space near the City complex.

McCabe spent much of the day browsing through newspaper articles in the city archives. He recalled hearing something about an FLDS group near Ruidoso, their leader having been arrested for welfare fraud. He couldn't find anything specific in the Santa Fe County area, but decided to explore another avenue. He gathered his notes and drove to Cerrillos, where he stopped by the feed store adjacent to the San Marcos Café and looked up an old friend whom everyone said was a font of information and knew most everything about the area. He parked in a shady spot on the side of the building.

A tall, thin man dressed in khaki coveralls, a baseball cap and heavy work boots greeted him as he alighted from the Hummer.

"Hey, McCabe, what brings you and that fancy vehicle out here? Don't tell me you've decided to stock that ranch of yours with a few head of cattle and you're here to buy a truckload of hay?" he said.

McCabe reached out and shook his hand. "My cow punching days are over, Bill, but I do have a few questions, and I know you're the answer guy around these parts," he said.

Bill wiped his face with a blue kerchief. "That's what they tell me. Pull up a chair and take a load off. What is it you're looking for?"

"You heard anything about a guy with multiple wives moving into this area? I swear I must be out of the loop on these things, having heard nothing myself other than that group out near Ruidoso."

"Yep, I remember that. Created quite a stir." Bill stroked the side of his beard. "Let me think for a minute. About six months ago a fellow came into the feed store to purchase some lumber. He said they were remodeling the old Buddhist compound in the mountains a little north of Kennedy Hill. I believe they were converting the place into a good-sized residence."

McCabe snapped his fingers. "I remember that place."

Bill nodded. "Yeah, it used to be some kind of New Age retreat. People from all over the place would go there to spend their time meditating and doing all that stuff these tree huggers are into," he said.

"Sounds about right," said McCabe.

"As I recall, the guy made a sizeable purchase. We delivered a couple of truckloads of lumber, along with a bunch of other supplies, cement, nails, and the like. The place is off County Road 69, kind of secluded, if you ask me, but it seems like they were looking for privacy more than anything else," Bill said.

McCabe gestured with his thumb. "I had some dealings last summer at Kennedy Hill serving papers. Lots of drug dealing going on. Kind of a rough place to settle down in, particularly if you have people traveling there to stay for an extended visit, don't you think?"

Bill reached into his back pocket for a tin of tobacco. He rolled out a cigarette, lit up and took a deep drag. "I hear most of them rogues have moved to greener pastures, if you know what I mean. The DFS 'copters haven't been buzzing around here for quite some time," he said.

"Know anything else about that place?" McCabe said.

"I recall just him and three or four women, and they kept to themselves while my guys were there. Didn't see any contractors around; looked like he was doing all the work himself. Women looked sturdy enough to be his helpers."

"Any name you can give me?"

Bill held up a finger. "Grab yourself a cup of java from the pot on the counter over there while I see what I can pull up on my laptop," he said. "Takes the internet a few minutes to boot up out here, no matter how many times we update these gizmos."

Ten minutes later, he returned to the table and handed McCabe a slip of paper. McCabe took a look, raised his eyebrows and folded the paper and slipped it into his pocket.

Bill blew a puff of smoke into the air. "Based on your reaction, was this what you were looking for?"

McCabe nodded. "Without going into detail, it's going to push us in a completely different direction in this case."

He thanked Bill and made his way to the Hummer. Before he called it a day, he had one more stop to make. He drove back into downtown Santa Fe and stopped at the County Courthouse where he obtained copies of property transactions in the Cerrillos area for the past year. By the time he had gathered everything he needed, it was already after seven. McCabe ran off some quick copies and figured he'd hook up with Romero on Monday.

Chapter Fifteen

——◆——

I T HAD BEEN over a week since the wedding and Jemimah had accomplished most of what she set out to do at the ranchette. The Monday morning light streamed through the bedroom as she awakened. She reached over to Romero's side and a piece of paper crackled as her hand touched the pillow. She hadn't stirred when he left for an early morning meeting with his staff. *Let the dog out. Didn't want to wake you. You were off somewhere in dreamland. Xoxo.*

The Border Collie peered through the door, then padded her way toward the bed and sat quietly next to the nightstand. When Jemimah stretched and reached for her robe, Molly's tail revved up, tapping against Jemimah's leg. She followed her owner into the kitchen and waited patiently while Jemimah made the coffee.

She set out Molly's food and water and headed into the bathroom. She hummed as she spread the foamy lather over her body and luxuriated under the hot shower. She was looking forward to resuming her job. Wrapped in a towel, she stood in front of her closet, and chuckled as she wondered what the big deal was about picking out an outfit to wear. Because of her promotion, she was happy to no longer be tied to the county's dress code of dark slacks and white tops, she reached in and grabbed a long-sleeved cotton blouse and a pair of tan slacks. Dressed and ready to go, she patted Molly on the head, telling her to be a good girl, watch the house and not be chasing Gato.

Traffic was light on the highway and she made it to St. Francis Drive in record time. Once downtown, she parked in the municipal parking lot near the Cathedral Basilica and stopped by the French Pastry Shop for a brioche and coffee. Cup in hand, she walked the block and then crossed San Francisco Street to the side entrance of her building. The County had renewed the lease on the office suite above the Plaza Café in downtown Santa Fe. She climbed the stairs and then felt her excitement increase as she strutted down the hallway toward her office. She was excited to be back on the job.

She unlocked the door and tapped the light switch, then walked across the room, pulled up the window shades and opened the windows and the glass-paned doors. She stood outside on the balcony, observing the hustle and bustle of the Santa Fe plaza. She took in a breath of fresh air, turned and walked back to the reception room. Not much had changed. It was as if she had never left.

Jemimah spent the morning arranging for internet and phone service, and finished up filling out the paperwork for her new position. She stocked her desk and the reception desk with supplies and loaded the printer and fax machine with paper. After lunch, she compiled a list of everything else she needed to requisition from the County warehouse to complete her move-in. Fortunately, most of her books and supplies had been stored in the corner cabinet and she stacked them in the bookcase.

By the end of day, every box was empty, and all office equipment was in its original place. Shelves and drawers were stocked with all the necessities to run an office. The cable guy had spent two long hours setting up the phone and internet connections, and had gabbed his way through the entire process. Feeling like a captive audience, Jemimah was relieved to see him go.

Her legs were sore from sitting cross-legged on the floor, but she was happy to have completed the task of setting up the old digs. There was no question in her mind that things were definitely looking up.

Chapter Sixteen

THE ELEVATOR SEEMED to drag as it lowered itself to the basement floor of the county morgue housed in the new judicial complex in downtown Santa Fe that Monday. Detective Romero exited the elevator and wound his way down the hallway toward the medical examiner's office. He stopped to press the intercom button and identified himself. The clerk buzzed him in and directed him to the third door on the right.

As he pushed through the door, the combined smells of formalin and alcohol assaulted his nostrils. The memory of the many autopsies he had attended in the past rushed back. It never got easier, and this was no exception. The last one was the most difficult. It was of a longtime acquaintance dating back to high school in Santa Fe, a mariachi whose body was found buried at the edge of a property near McCabe's ranch in Cerrillos. It was tough enough to attend an autopsy not knowing the victim, but twice so when the deceased was familiar.

When Romero entered the room, the assistant handed him a large paper bag containing a green plastic gown, shoe covers, a hair cap, latex gloves and surgical mask, all disposable. She pointed in the direction of the bathrooms. After Romero donned the garments, he was directed to the last table in the rear section, where he walked past stainless steel counters, aluminum gurneys, x-ray illuminators and a host of other shiny objects, all flooded with light from rows of bright fluorescent lights overhead. Romero felt a chill run through his spine as he wondered if he would ever get used to the picture of death. He pulled a small blue jar from his pocket and unscrewed the lid. A dab of Noxzema cream on his nostrils did little to erase the noxious smells.

He was surprised to see Dr. Harry Donlon at the helm of this autopsy, who greeted him with the usual sneer, peering at him through bifocals which balanced near the tip of his nose. Donlon had proven himself to be one of the most annoying and arbitrary individuals Romero had the displeasure of having contact with. Although skilled at his profession, he lacked courtesy, compassion and people skills in general.

"Detective Romero, surprised to see you're still in law enforcement. Didn't think you had the stomach for it," he said.

"I could say the same of you, Harry. I thought you had retired and gone off to live on some island far away from here, as I recall, preferably one without any brown people," Romero said, recalling the streak of bigotry Donlon expressed with little encouragement against Hispanics, Native Americans, Blacks and other cultures.

Donlon huffed. "I am retired, but these people are so backed up that if I didn't step in to take care of things, they'll never catch up. That new fellow they hired doesn't know his butt from a hole in the ground. Of course, they didn't ask me for my recommendation, so the County will have to deal with that misfire on their own."

From previous experience, Romero knew it best to keep silent, rather than encourage the tirade which would surely follow if he offered a comment or opinion. He took his place behind the observation shield and took a deep breath.

The ME motioned to his assistant. "Let's get this show on the road, kid." He fiddled with the mike attached to his lapel and then recited the usual spiel about the purpose of an autopsy, stating the obvious. This was followed by information about the victim's age, height, sex and race. "This examination follows a series of tests on the victim, including total body X-rays, DNA and tox tests and a complete external exam."

The assistant noted the date, time, and names of those in attendance, and recorded every word Donlon uttered, including the distasteful ones.

The ME slid an x-ray film over the light box and pointed to a spot. "Bullet completely shattered the left side of the skull. Death was immediate. Bloodwork showed nothing out of the ordinary, elevated HDL, A1C, probably mild diabetic, nothing serious. Aside from being a little overweight, it appears he was in pretty good shape." He dropped the bullet into the metal pan. His assistant placed it in a plastic bag.

Donlon tipped his head in Romero's direction. "It appears to be suitable for ballistic comparison."

He flipped a page on the clipboard. "My, my. I see from the file that this fellow here is a Mormon. I wonder how many wives will be attending his funeral."

Romero rolled his eyes. *Same old asshole. No respect for the dead, or the living, for that matter.* He saw no need to correct the wife remark.

After a long hour of cutting, dissecting and probing, followed by innumerable off-color comments, the autopsy was finally concluded. From body temperature tests taken at the site where the body was discovered, Donlon determined the time of death to be no less than forty-eight hours before he was found at approximately 9:00 AM Sunday. This would set the time of death at some time Friday morning.

"This was pretty cut and dry. There are no wounds or bruises to the body, no defense wounds, no indication that a struggle of any sort preceded the death. Definitely not suicide, by any means. Cause of death is a single small caliber bullet entered through the left side of the head, fractured the skull and lodged in the ear canal, probably causing instantaneous death, or as is the case in most of these situations, the poor guy never knew what hit him."

Donlon handed the plastic evidence bag containing the bullet to Romero. Then, with his usual theatrics, the aged coroner peeled off his mask and the rest of his protective gear, tossed it in the Hazmat can, and bounded out of the room.

Romero checked himself out with Security, and made his way through the complex out to the parking lot where his cruiser was parked. He leaned up against the fender of his vehicle and breathed a sigh of relief. He lit up a cigarette, taking long deep drags, then crushed the butt into a rock and pulled himself into the driver's side. He knew it would take a while to shake off the after effects of the autopsy.

Chapter Seventeen

————◆————

O N THE WAY back to his vehicle, Romero checked the time and realized he had only a few minutes to get to the courthouse. He was scheduled to testify for the DA on a recent drug bust. He drove through downtown and up the ramp of the parking garage adjacent to the courthouse and booked it across the lot and through the main doors of the District Court building. The security guard rushed him through just in time.

Testimony complete, the DA shook Romero's hand. He waved at the security guard and signed out of the building. He was approaching the parking garage when he ran into Tim McCabe.

"Hey, McCabe, what are you doing around here? I was just thinking of calling you for lunch. You got time?" Romero said.

"That sounds like a plan. Missed breakfast this morning. I don't care where, as long as it's smothered in chile," McCabe said.

"There's a new place over at DeVargas Mall, The Atrisco Café & Bar. Been wanting to try it," Romero said. "I hear they serve lumberjack portions of Mexican food. Nobody goes away without adding another notch to their belt."

"Sounds good to me. I'll meet you there. Need to drop

something off at the post office first," McCabe said.

Fifteen minutes later they were seated at a booth in a corner of the restaurant whose name loosely translated to *near the waters*, perhaps a reference to the tail end of the Santa Fe River which ran parallel to the mall road. A bright red chile ristra hung from a heavy post near the long bar which ran across the side underneath a heavy beamed ceiling where patrons sat on stools. Romero ordered the grilled lamb burrito and McCabe ordered the red enchilada plate topped with a fried egg. Both were deep in conversation when the waitress arrived with their plates and big glasses of iced tea.

McCabe gave him a quick capsule of the information he had gathered last Friday. They decided to take a quick trip out to Kennedy Hill to check out the situation.

"I can take a look at the paperwork on the drive out," Romero said between mouthfuls. "Tim, you didn't answer my question about what you were doing at the courthouse," he said.

McCabe set his fork down. "Oh, that. I had just signed off on a restraining order against a guy from Texas. He's been bombarding me with emails, some of them a little dicey," McCabe said.

"Are these related to the treasure hunt? I thought someone would have found it by now," Romero said.

McCabe gestured with his hand. "Started off that way, and then the SOB shows up at my house last week and wouldn't leave. He kept taking photos of the house and the yard. Laura and our housekeeper were pretty shook up. They had called 911 but by the time I arrived home, he was gone."

Romero whistled. "That sounds pretty nasty, McCabe. You got enough security in place?"

"Oh yeah, for sure, but that doesn't keep someone away who's crafty and determined," he said. "I might need to post a guard at the entry. That eight foot wall used to deter intruders, but these days hackers can come up with the combination to swing the gates open."

"I hear you. Nothing's impenetrable anymore," Romero said.

McCabe dipped a blue corn chip into the bowl of salsa. "It irks me to have this happening. That wasn't our initial purpose. Our aim was to not only share the wealth, but to get families out in the fresh air. Hundreds of fathers have taken their kids out, and they love it. Unfortunately, there are always crazies out there who ruin it for everyone."

"You should see some of these emails. I have to snicker when the media says it's an *alleged* treasure chest hidden somewhere in the Rocky Mountains," McCabe said.

Romero nodded. "It was sure as hell real to me. I remember Jemimah and I searched a few areas ourselves on our way to Yellowstone last year. Whoever finds it better have a nose like a hound dog."

"Some guy posted on Facebook that the treasure was really stashed in a tree in my front yard. Go figure. Maybe that's what prompted this fellow to drop by my house unannounced," McCabe said.

"I'm sure your fans outnumber the naysayers," Romero said.

"That might be true, but unfortunately I've had to deal with more than a few shady and unwelcome characters. I'm pretty sure this guy I'm trying to get a restraining order on is responsible for a slew of threatening emails."

"Have you been able to track them? I can get one of the guys to help you out there," Romero said.

"So far, my computer guru has narrowed the IP address down to somewhere in Southern Colorado. Unfortunately, the location covers a wide area and will probably end up pinpointing a computer in a Kinko's store," he said. "I'm doubly annoyed that this would happen right before I'm scheduled to be in New York for another TV promotion on a daytime talk show to give out another clue."

Romero pushed his plate to the side and motioned to the waitress for the ticket. "Well, let me know how things turn out.

I'm sure you're capable of protecting your family, but you call me if anything comes up. I'll be at your door before you hang the phone up," Romero said.

McCabe reached into his pocket. "Laura and I both carry these little security gadgets. An old colleague of mine is in the process of releasing them to the public, and we volunteered to be his guinea pigs." He pointed to the small plastic square. "See, it's kind of a micro cell phone and can pick up your location in a fifty mile grid."

Romero grinned. "Sounds like a handy gadget to have, but what are the chances of an experienced officer like yourself getting lost in the woods."

"That's true, but imagine an oldster wandering off from a nursing home, or a parent losing a kid in a shopping mall. These could be invaluable."

"Tim, all kidding aside. I'm really sorry you're having to go through this. Let me know if there's any way I can help alleviate some of that extra stress sitting on your shoulders," Romero said.

McCabe took a last sip from his glass. "Thanks, Rick. I appreciate that. The next step I have to take is to see if the judge is going to sign the restraining order before I take off and hope that once it's in effect, the guy will stay away. That won't happen until the judge reviews my petition, and who knows how long that will take."

As they exited the restaurant, Romero couldn't help but notice the creases across McCabe's forehead. He could tell his friend was more concerned about the situation than he was letting on.

Out in the parking lot, McCabe turned to Romero. "Let's take my vehicle out there. That police cruiser of yours is likely to give someone a heart attack if they see us coming down the pike."

Romero chuckled. "You're probably right. I'll drop my car off and then we can head out."

On the way back to the substation, Romero dropped by

the lab and logged the bullet from the autopsy into evidence. The tech ran a quick test and informed him that because of the rifling on the slug removed from the victim's body, he was fairly certain the marks were consistent with ammunition used in a Glock 9mm. pistol.

Chapter Eighteen

Romero pulled into the substation a few minutes behind McCabe. He eased the cruiser into his space and reached for his service revolver before alarming the vehicle and hustling over to McCabe's vehicle. He lifted himself up into the passenger seat of the blue Hummer and secured the seat belt as he looked around the interior. "You must spend a few hours a week keeping this baby clean. Always looks like you just drove it off the lot."

"That's Laura's doing. She has our housekeeper run the shop vac through it at least once a week. I've learned to not leave anything on the floorboard or it will get sucked up."

Romero laughed. "Wish I could say the same. The floorboard on my cruiser has become a receptacle for every slip of paper that runs through my fingers in a week's time. Every few days I gather it all up and give it to Clarissa so she can save the pertinent stuff and toss the rest."

"That's quite a bookkeeping system you have there, Rick."

"I'm sure a few months with my new wife will change that," he said. "She's a stickler for keeping things in order."

McCabe reached over and handed him the file containing all the information he gathered the prior afternoon. Romero was glancing through it when McCabe interrupted his train of thought.

"This is all in the papers I handed you, but the guy's name is Jason Hodge. Bought the property a while back. County records indicate he hails from a small town near Provo, Utah," McCabe said, looking for a reaction.

"Lots of people with that last name, especially from Utah," Romero said, flipping through the remainder of the file. "Great job gathering info, Tim."

They wound their way toward Kennedy Hill, a small burg in the knolls southeast of Cerrillos, just this side of the County line. The village was nestled between the Ortiz Mountains and Galisteo Creek. There was only one way in, and it was originally a U.S. Forest Service road. The steep hills and rutted roads made for slow going. Up ahead, nestled against a hill they could see a number of buildings. What appeared to be the main house of the compound was located at the end of a gravel road. It was a two story building topped with a blue tin roof, á *la* Northern New Mexico style.

As they rounded the turn, they could see there were actually four identical buildings separated by a one story building in the center. Several outbuildings stood on the left, and a creek ran nearby. The area was surrounded by a lightly wooded section with mature cottonwoods and pine trees. Facing them on the west side was a long portal overlooking a lush green lawn enclosed by a low adobe wall. A flagstone path led to an oversized wood door. The grounds were neatly manicured, with colorful foliage set against the house. The entire picture appeared to be a well-planned work-in-progress.

McCabe pulled into the horseshoe shaped gravel drive and parked. Before he could kill the ignition, a woman stepped out of the first building and approached the driver's side of the vehicle. Dressed in a gingham shirt and dark trousers, her hair was neatly pulled back in a ponytail. She was holding a leaf rake in her hands.

"May I help you?" she said.

The two men stepped out of the vehicle. "Yes, Ma'am. We're here to see a Mr. Jason Hodge, is he available?"

She had a perplexed look on her face. "We don't get many visitors out here. Are you neighbors?"

He held out his badge. "No, we are not. Let me introduce myself. I am Detective Rick Romero from the Santa Fe County Sheriff's Office. This is Deputy Tim McCabe."

McCabe tipped his hat.

Her hands went to her cheek. "Sheriff's Department? Is there some trouble? We have all the building permits we need."

"Ma'am, we are here to see Mr. Hodge. Is he available?" Romero repeated.

She turned in the direction of the barn. "I believe he's out back somewhere. I'll go get him. You can wait inside. The wind seems to be picking up."

They followed her through the front door into a large living room. Tall, narrow windows ushered in an abundance of natural light, which gave the room an almost churchlike appearance. The house smelled of an odd combination of Pine-Sol and freshly baked bread.

"Can I get you anything to drink? I have some sun tea brewing," she said.

"We're fine, thank you," Romero said.

She pointed to the sofa. "Please have a seat. Wait here and I'll go get Jason. I shouldn't be too long, although sometimes he's down at the creek hauling water." She disappeared though the door in the back.

Five minutes had elapsed when a man Romero assumed was Jason Hodge came down the hallway. He was about six foot tall, with steel-blue eyes and sandy brown hair peppered with a touch of gray. He was dressed in blue jeans, a checkered shirt with rolled-up sleeves and a sawdust covered apron. From the description provided by Eliza Simpson, Romero decided this was the same person.

Romero stood. "Jason Hodge, I presume?"

"Yes, what can I do for you?"

Romero introduced himself, McCabe nodded. "I hope we're not interrupting your work. Looks like you're doing a bit of construction," he said.

"That's all right, I was about due for a short break," he said.

Romero handed him a business card. "Mr. Hodge, Deputy McCabe and I are with the Santa Fe County Sheriff's Office. We're investigating a matter involving a Lawrence Tanner from Provo, Utah."

Hodge untied his apron and set it on the chair. "And might I ask how that concerns me?"

"Do you know Mr. Tanner?" Romero said.

"I believe I might have met the gentleman, once or twice when we resided in Utah," he said.

"Did you have occasion to meet with him here in Santa Fe or anywhere in New Mexico recently?" Romero asked.

"No, I did not. Don't remember the last time I saw him, but it certainly wasn't recently, and it wasn't in New Mexico," Hodge said.

"Under what circumstances had you met him in the past, was it a friendly meeting?" Romero said.

"Mr. Tanner and I had a disagreement at one point in time. It never went beyond an exchange of a few harsh words." He took a long swallow of water. "What the hell does that have to do with anything?"

"Would you mind telling me where you were on Friday morning of last week?" Romero said.

Hodge glanced at the calendar on the wall. "That would be May 12th. I was here, as I have been for weeks, trying to put the final touches on the barn. I'm doing most of the work myself." He paused. "If this is going to take much longer, let's have a seat. I've been on my feet since before sunrise." He directed them to the dining room, where they sat down on the long benches on each side of the table.

"All right, Mr. Hodge, let me continue," Romero said. "Is there anyone here who can verify your whereabouts on that day?"

Hodge crossed his arms in front of his chest. "Detective, I have four women here who can vouch for my whereabouts, not only for that day but probably for the hundred days preceding that. There's always one of them present at one time or another," he said.

"Could we speak to one or more of them?" Romero said.

McCabe leaned forward. "And while we're waiting, do you mind if I have a look at your driver's license?"

Hodge reached into his back pocket and retrieved his wallet. He flipped through the cards and pulled out his license. "Not at all. I haven't yet changed it over to New Mexico, though. I believe I still have a couple of months."

McCabe nodded. "Do you mind if I take a photograph?"

Hodge frowned. "Would it make a difference if I did? I suppose it will be all right." He stood and faced Romero. "Excuse me, I'll bring in one of the women."

A short time later he returned to the room, followed by three women. "I don't know where Clara is, probably out back watering the garden, but these three should suffice."

Hodge introduced each of them. "Hannah Rebecca, Kathryn, and Brigid. These gentlemen are from the Sheriff's Office in Santa Fe. They'd like to ask a few questions."

Romero noted their names. "Hannah Rebecca, we'll start with you. Can you tell me where Mr. Hodge was last Friday?" He said.

"Yes, of course I can," she said. "He was here at the house, with us, working on the barn. I think he worked on the south wall, setting up the two by fours. We keep a progress journal. If you like I can check that to make sure."

"Maybe at a later time. And as far as you know, did he leave the premises at any time during that day, even for a short time?" Romero said.

"No, not in the morning, I'm sure he didn't. He was waiting for a delivery truck to bring some more lumber, but the driver got lost and said he would try again the next day, which he did. On Fridays, we always go into town to do our shopping. We take the van and shop at the Smith's grocery store on the south side of Cerrillos Road. I can dig up the credit card receipt he signed if that's necessary."

Romero turned to the other women. "Do you both agree?"

Kathryn nodded and Brigid answered. "Yes, our husband was present then and has been for the last week. He only takes time off to have a meal or to sleep, and then he's back at it."

"*Our* husband?" Romero already knew the answer but thought he would ask anyway.

"Jason has four wives. It is an acceptable practice in our religion," she said.

"Out of curiosity, what religion is that, might I inquire?"

"We are members of the FLDS, the Fundamentalist Church of Jesus Christ of Latter Day Saints," she said proudly.

The term had been explained to Romero by the bishop, so he didn't expound on the question.

Jason Hodge stood and took a step forward. "Now, can you tell me what this is all about? I have work to do and I'd like to get back to it."

"Last Sunday a body was found a couple of miles south of here," McCabe said. "It appears to be a homicide."

"What does that have to do with us? Or me in particular?" Hodge retorted.

"We have information that you may have had an altercation with the victim in the past," Romero said.

Hodge returned to his seat and clasped his hands in front of him. His exasperation was evident to the detective. "Exactly who is this victim?"

Romero produced a photo from his suit pocket and slid it across the table. "Lawrence Tanner, the man I mentioned earlier."

The wife named Brigid clutched her chest and gasped audibly. The two other wives helped her to a nearby chair.

Chapter Nineteen

BRIGID HODGE'S FACE turned ashen. Her hands began to shake. "My God, are you saying that Lawrence is dead?"

Jason Hodge stiffened. "I didn't know the man well, but I'm sorry to hear that. What happened, if I might ask?"

"I can't give you any particulars at the moment. Suffice it to say that he was found dead in the woods not too far from here," Romero said. "Your compound is only a couple of miles south."

"I don't see how that would involve any of us," Hodge said.

"Can I ask why one of your wives reacted so strongly?" Romero said.

She stifled a sob and Hodge answered for her. "Lawrence Tanner is her ex-husband."

Romero turned to face Brigid. "Is that right, Mrs. Hodge?"

She clutched the arm of the chair. "Yes, but I haven't had any contact with him for the last six months, before we moved to New Mexico." She was having a difficult time controlling her emotions. "Would you excuse me," she said. "I have things to finish, as do my sister wives."

Romero assured her the conversation could resume at another time. The three wives rushed down the hallway. He turned back to Hodge. "All right, Mr. Hodge. A few more questions and we'll be out of your hair. Can I ask if you own any firearms?"

"No, I do not. We don't believe in violence. I don't own a firearm. Never have," he said. "And I'm certain my wives do not either."

"Do you mind if McCabe here takes a look around?" Romero was keenly aware that unless an individual agreed, looking through their private property without a warrant was unacceptable.

Hodge waved his arm across his chest. "Detective, we have nothing to hide. You are welcome to walk through all four houses, if you like."

"That probably won't be necessary," said McCabe, as he headed through the corridor. He knew that someone giving permission so quickly rarely had anything they didn't want seen. He stuck his head into the neat-as-a-pin bedrooms, each closet with nothing out of place, filled with neatly pressed shirts and blue jeans. Shoes and boots occupied the racks on the bottom. The medicine cabinets in the bathrooms held the usual assortment of generic remedies and grooming aids. Every additional room was also in just been cleaned condition. The kitchens were cavernous and furnished with stainless steel appliances, long wooden tables and benches. Each pantry was well stocked with staples, rice, canned goods and such.

He walked across the gravel driveway to the second and third houses. Before he returned to the main kitchen to regroup with Romero, he made his way through the yard and into the barn. He noted that even there, everything was neatly in place.

On the way back to the main house, he passed by an outdoor shed and poked his head in, expecting to see more of the same. As he surmised, the shed was filled to capacity with construction equipment, gardening tools and wheelbarrows, but McCabe caught a glimpse of something that to his trained eye seemed out of place.

In one corner on a shelf behind the post digger was an

object wrapped in a folded yellow terrycloth face towel. He moved the tools aside and lifted a corner of the towel with his pen. Underneath was a 9 mm. Glock pistol. McCabe slipped on a pair of gloves, inserted the pen through the trigger guard and smelled the barrel. It appeared to have been fired recently. He ejected the magazine, pulled back the slide and the cartridge from the chamber popped out. He made sure the safety trigger was on. He replaced the firearm back between the fold of the towel and carried the wrapped weapon back to the main house.

Detective Romero and Jason Hodge both looked up as McCabe entered the room.

"What do you have there, Tim?" Romero said.

McCabe placed the revolver, still wrapped in the towel, on the table in front of the two men. He lifted the side to expose the weapon. "Looks like a Glock G-26 subcompact, designed for conceal and carry. One round used, nine remained in the magazine."

Hodge's eyes bulged and he crossed his arms. "Where did you get that?"

"Found it in the shed behind the second house," McCabe said.

"I hate to disappoint you, detectives, but I don't know where that came from," Hodge said.

"Are you saying this weapon doesn't belong to you, Mr. Hodge?" Romero said.

"I'm saying exactly that. I told you I don't own a firearm and never have," he said. "This must be some kind of a joke."

"Do you have any idea how it would have gotten into that shed?" McCabe said.

His back stiffened. "Of course not. I've never seen that before. I don't know what I need to say to convince you. It is not mine, and I can assure you it certainly doesn't belong to any of my wives."

Romero was aware that ballistic tests conducted by the crime lab had confirmed the weapon used in the homicide was a 9mm pistol, probably a Glock. He knew the serial number on this one might not be traceable, as was usually the case in matters of homicide.

Hodge looked first at Romero and then at McCabe. "You people don't seriously think I would be stupid enough to kill someone and then hide the weapon in plain sight, do you?"

Romero stood. "Stranger things have happened, Mr. Hodge. I'm going to ask you to come downtown with us. We'd like to ask you a few more questions," he said.

Hodge's face turned white. "What? You can't be serious! Am I under arrest?"

"I'm afraid so, turn around and put your hands behind you." McCabe unstrapped a set of Flexi-cuffs from his belt and wrapped them around Hodge's wrists and Mirandized him.

In a panic, two of the wives ran into the room and pulled on McCabe's arm. "What are you doing? What's going on?"

Hodge shook his head. "It's all right. I'm accompanying these gentlemen downtown to clear this up. There has to be a mistake," Hodge said.

The hysterical women watched as Romero escorted Hodge out to the vehicle and secured him in the back seat, then pulled himself onto the adjoining seat. McCabe drove down the winding road to its intersection with Highway 14, and then drove to the substation. They transferred Hodge into the back of the police cruiser, which was better equipped than the Hummer for transporting prisoners. Romero didn't think there would be a problem, but he wanted to follow protocol. McCabe followed closely behind.

Twenty minutes later, they arrived at the County Jail next to the Sheriff's Department where Hodge was taken to an interview room. On the way into town, Romero anticipated that Hodge might exercise his rights to an attorney, which would bring any interrogation to a halt. He was not surprised when Hodge did exactly that; he was booked on suspicion of murder. It was after seven when Romero drove home.

Chapter Twenty

JEMIMAH HEARD GRAVEL crunching on the driveway and pulled the curtain back on the living room window to see Romero's cruiser parked in the driveway. For the next five minutes, she watched as he sat without moving and figured he was already working too hard and probably exhausted. Romero reached over the seat for his briefcase and strode down the path to the porch. The embrace he gave Jemimah as he walked through the door lasted for a few long moments. She held him at arm's length.

"Looks like you had a long day."

He wiggled out of his windbreaker and hung it in the hall closet. "McCabe and I had some inquiries to conduct in the area. It was already too late to go back to the office and I know I promised earlier we could have an early dinner and maybe catch a movie. Probably a little late for that," he said.

She reached up and put her hand on his cheek. "I'm sure we can throw something together. The fridge is full. You seem a bit distracted. Everything going okay at work?"

He shrugged his shoulders. "I guess this latest homicide has suddenly gotten under my skin."

"I know how frustrating it can be when things move slowly.

Anything of substance show up?"

"Not much," he said. He was silent for a moment and thought about how to broach the subject. "No, that's not right. Jem, sit down, I think we need to talk."

She looked at him, a surprised look on her face. "This sounds serious."

He pulled her toward the couch. "Yes, I think it is."

Again he struggled to pull his thoughts together, strings of words running through his mind. He thought again about exactly how he was going to tell her. Maybe he should just blurt it out, or maybe he should wait until a better time.

Jemimah put her hand on his arm. His hesitation made her more nervous about whatever he was trying to tell her. It wasn't like him to beat around the bush.

"Rick, you're starting to scare me. What's going on?"

"I guess there's no easy way to say this, Jem."

She started to speak. He put his finger on her lips. "I need to ask you a few questions, and they might sound odd, but hear me out. Tell me again the name of the town where you were born," he said.

"Hildale, Utah, just outside of Salt Lake City. Why?"

He raised his finger. "Bear with me, Jem. And could you tell me what your parents' names are?"

Jemimah took a deep breath. "My father's name is Jason Hodge, and my mother's name is Clara Wells Hodge."

He took her hands in his. "You know I've never pressed you about your childhood, and I understand your wanting to keep this information to yourself, but right now I need to know these things."

"I think you know a lot about me," she said. "We've known each other for a couple of years now."

"But I don't know enough. I have never asked for details about your life, knowing that you would be forthcoming if you felt there was anything you wanted to share," he said.

"So why are these questions important now?"

He got up from the couch, walked over to the cabinet and

poured two glasses of Scotch whiskey. He handed Jemimah one and sat down on the hassock in front of her. "I think you're going to need this."

A wide-eyed Jemimah looked deeply into her husband's eyes as he leaned forward and took her hand in his. "There's really no way to say this. You know this recent homicide I've been working on?"

"Yes, the guy found under a sleeping bag somewhere east of Cerrillos?"

"That would be it. Unfortunately, this is going to hit close to home. McCabe and I made an arrest today of a man who we suspect might be involved," Romero said.

"And?"

He sighed. "And I believe the man is your father, Jason Hodge."

He felt her hand tightening on his. "That can't be, Rick! Are you certain? That's a fairly common name. Besides, they would never leave Utah. How do you know it's my father? I haven't seen him in years, and what's he doing in New Mexico?"

He stroked her cheek. "I know how difficult this must be for you. To answer your question, from his driver's license and other information we've compiled," he said. "I'm pretty sure."

The couple sat in silence. As if sensing something was amiss, the Border collie jumped on the couch and put her head in Jemimah's lap. She absentmindedly smoothed the dog's fur.

She turned to face him. "This is too bizarre, Rick. Tell me everything."

He explained what had occurred earlier in the day, about how he had spoken to the fiancée of the victim who had arrived in Santa Fe to make arrangements for the body, and of McCabe gathering info about an FLDS family who had moved into the area near Kennedy Hill. He concluded by detailing their visit to the compound, meeting the wives, the finding of the weapon and the resulting arrest.

"We both know that a huge percentage of homicide victims knew their killers. That usually serves to provide us with a decent pool of potential suspects right off the bat. Might be a bit different here, since the victim is from out of state, but the suspect formerly resided in that state," he said.

Jemimah listened quietly, taking in his every word.

Weeks before, Romero had attended a seminar on advanced interrogation techniques at the NM Law Enforcement Academy. He did not recall it covering a suspect who might very well be your father-in-law.

"I know this is putting the cart before the horse, but unfortunately, Jem, because of your position, it's probably going to fall on you to interview the witnesses. Dealing with this case might bring back a lot of unpleasant memories. Are you going to be able to do that objectively?" He asked.

She absentmindedly rubbed the nape of her neck. "I'm aware of that, Rick, but you know I'm no good about sitting on the sidelines. This is a homicide case; my job is to conduct witness interviews and tender my opinion. I don't really know any of these people who might come forward. Like most of the witnesses I've interviewed all these years, they are strangers to me."

Romero heard a tiny crack in her voice, the one she tried to cover up with a forced cough. He could never understand why she always struggled to keep her emotions tucked away. In the past he was used to Chicana chicks who expressed every single emotion by screaming or crying. He knew his wife was putting on a brave face for his benefit, and couldn't even fathom the turmoil that must be going on inside that beautiful head of hers. He wished there was some way he could protect her, but knew that wasn't even remotely possible. "It's getting late. Let me see what I can throw together for a quick dinner." He walked toward the kitchen and rifled through the cupboards.

While the chicken stew simmered, he stood in the doorway of the kitchen, his gaze on Jemimah, who had collapsed into the easy chair by the fireplace. He crossed the room and pulled the leather hassock closer and sat in front of her, their knees touching.

She ran her fingers though her hair. "My God, Rick, I think I'm in shock. I keep wanting to ask again, are you sure, but I know if there's no doubt in your mind, then there shouldn't be one in mine." Her chest heaved.

"I'm so sorry, Jem. It's a pretty tough way to receive the news. I couldn't see any other way around it." He cradled his arms around her. "Just let me hold you. I don't think I can come up with the right words to be of any comfort."

She squeezed his arm. "My sentiments exactly." She leaned on his shoulder and closed her eyes. Memories flooded back of the last time Jemimah saw her father. The aroma of food cooking on the stove brought on a sudden wave of nausea.

Chapter Twenty-One

THE LOCAL MEDIA had a field day. Readers were used to perusing news articles about arrests for petty thefts, DWIs, texting while driving and a host of other small but time-consuming crimes. This was a very big deal. The Tuesday morning headlines from the Santa Fe New Mexican and the Albuquerque Journal North stared out at Jemimah. *Polygamous suspect kills rival in fit of rage.* The scandalous article went on to say that Jason Hodge had allegedly shot the victim and left him for dead just two miles from the compound which he and his harem of wives occupied in Kennedy Hill near the village of Cerrillos. Detective Romero was reported as having no comment and adding that the body had been recently discovered and the case was under investigation. It was too early to make a judgment.

On the Channel Thirteen early news, the reporter indicated the evidence against the suspect appeared circumstantial, but as most listeners knew, many a defendant had been tried and convicted with less evidence than was currently available in the case.

Based on her own experience, Jemimah knew that in some cases the term circumstantial evidence was a convenient theory. Try the first person they suspect and the case is over. It appeared that something similar was happening here. After all, there was always backlash directed at polygamous families in any setting. That was one of the reasons they stayed primarily in states like Utah and Colorado and did their best to stay out of the limelight. New Mexico was proving to be less accepting than she knew they expected.

She dropped her reading glasses to her nose and looked at the photo of her father. His hair was short, salt and pepper, neatly trimmed. He had not changed much over the years. He appeared tanned, trim and muscular. Jemimah could see why these women would be attracted to him. If she didn't know him, she would never suspect he was nearing sixty. She leaned back in her chair and had a bizarre thought. *What if he is guilty?* It was difficult enough looking in from the sidelines. She wondered if she needed to muster up the courage to see him. *Hell,* she didn't know how he would react, and *double hell,* she didn't know how *she* would react. She decided she would leave things as they were.

Earlier that morning she had received a call from Sheriff Medrano. "Dr. Hodge, I was just informed by Detective Romero that the suspect in this homicide is your father and that you have connections to his family. Is that true?"

"Yes, it is true that he's my father, but I have had no contact with any of them for over twenty years. I left the family home when I was a teenager and never returned," she said.

"My concern is that there might be some legal ramification about your questioning someone who could conceivably be familiar to you," he continued.

"I can assure you, Sheriff, that since the suspect has opted for legal representation, no interrogation or interview of him will be allowed. As far as the wives go, they are essentially strangers to me and I would treat them the same as the hundreds of interviews I have conducted over the years.

"I will take extra measures to assure there will be no problem," Jemimah said.

"All right," he said. "This is a sensitive situation and I need your assurance that you can handle these witness interviews without your personal feelings influencing the outcome in any manner."

Jemimah assured him her participation would be completely professional, regardless of the circumstances.

She tossed the newspapers into the recycle bin and gathered up the breakfast dishes. She glanced at the clock on the microwave and hurried to throw herself together for work. Half hour later, she was ready to go and made it through the morning traffic without incident. No yellow barrels, snarled traffic or speed traps.

Seated at her desk, she sipped on a container of coffee. As she anticipated would happen, Jemimah struggled with the thought of meeting the women, since two of them were strongly connected to her childhood. But she had a job to do and she was going to do it. She looked at the notes Detective Romero had provided and reached for her phone. She dialed the number and tapped her fingers on the desk while it rang.

After a few rings, a voice she didn't recognize answered. "This is Dr. Hodge with the Santa Fe County Sheriff's Office. To whom am I speaking?" she said.

"This is Brigid. How may I help you? Is this about Jason?" she said. "Is he all right?"

Jemimah stiffened at the mention of her father and the woman's concern. "I'm calling to set up a convenient time when each of you can come to my office for an interview," she said.

"Oh, yes, the detective mentioned someone would be calling to do that. I guess we can make ourselves available at any time," she said.

Jemimah glanced at her Daybook. "Would this coming Friday at ten work for you? I can have my assistant email you directions to my office."

"We don't have a strong internet connection out here, but I can take the information down. Just let me get something to write with. Do you want all four of us to come at the same time?" She said.

Four?! Jemimah said to herself.

"Hello, are you still there?" the woman on the other end of the line said.

Jemimah cleared her throat. "Yes, I'm sorry. Certainly you can come together, but I would want to interview each of you separately, if that's not a problem," she said. "You can call my assistant if there's any change." Jemimah rattled off the number.

Brigid jotted down the directions. "All right, we will be there."

Jemimah instructed her to park in the City parking lot across the street, which was more accessible, said goodbye and then hung up the phone. She stared at her appointment book, making a mental note that this wife had apparently not made the connection to Jemimah's last name.

***

DETECTIVE ROMERO STEPPED out through the French doors of his office onto the small patio which was profuse with the scent of blooming lilacs. He stretched out his arms and took a deep breath. "Damn, this day has been dragging along," he said to himself, and pulled a pack of cigarettes from his chest pocket and lit up. He had promised Jemimah he would stop smoking, but recent pressures from the brass made it an easy promise to forget. His earlier meeting with the crime techs had produced no worthwhile information on the homicide they were working. He reached for his cell phone and dialed McCabe.

"Tim, I've been going over the lab reports after my meeting with the techs earlier today. What do you think of this?" He read a passage from the document: 'The victim's shoes had a sticky residue on the soles and pine needles stuck to the indentations.' The lab says the substance has the same characteristics as pine pitch."

McCabe took a moment. "They're probably right. A lot of the pine and piñon trees in the area surrounding my property have this sticky stuff that oozes from the trunks at certain times of the year."

"Oh, yeah, I remember when we were kids our parents took us piñon picking, this amber colored substance used to stick to our hands. It was hell to get off and we had to soak our fingers in turpentine," Romero said.

"That's the one. The Spanish call it *trementina*. I saw something on PBS where they said local craftsmen gather it in containers to make a type of varnish for their retablos and bultos, traditional painted panels and woodcarvings that you see in the museum gift shops and at Spanish Market each year," McCabe said.

"Is this stuff common to all wooded areas?" Romero said.

"Not as far as I know, just in certain northern elevations. The victim might have been hiking or walking in the woods near where he was found a few miles from the compound, maybe up the side of the mountain before it tapered off into the valley. Did the techs indicate this stuff showed up on their foot covers as they inspected the scene?"

"Come to think of it, there's no mention of that. That's a good point, McCabe. I think we need to make another visit out to the crime scene and see if we can pull something out of the hat. Crime techs said they're done on the site, but you never know if they missed something," Romero said.

"I'll swing by and pick you up, amigo," McCabe said.

Chapter Twenty-Two

————— ❖ —————

THE SKIES HAD darkened as McCabe pulled into the substation parking lot, where Detective Romero waited. The drive to the crime scene was a short fifteen minutes and the gathering of clouds threatened to engulf them in a stormy monsoon, months before the predicted season. The dirt road off the highway had received just enough moisture to tamp down the dust, but nothing more. McCabe pulled off the road and parked next to a grove of salt cedars. They headed toward a marked trail just north of the vehicle.

McCabe looked down at Romero's shoes. "Those dress shoes weren't designed for this terrain, Rick."

"Yeah, I need to watch my step. Dress code aside, this is one of those days where boots and jeans would work a lot better," he said.

A short hike later, they reached the site, where the yellow tape wound around the trees now flapped in the breeze. The area was far enough away from the road where sounds off in the distance were nonexistent. It was eerily quiet.

McCabe walked the perimeter of one side and Detective Romero walked the other. Each took samples of the ground fifty to a hundred feet in each direction, and met back at the center, where they marked the evidence bags and then checked the bottoms of their shoes.

"Just as I thought," Romero said. "The sticky residue seems to be present about fifty feet from the scene, and where the body was found, it is almost nonexistent."

"That would mean that our killer might have traversed the same areas, probably following a short distance behind the victim where they wouldn't be spotted," said McCabe.

"Makes sense to me. Because there's such a thick ground cover around here, the techs wouldn't have found much in the form of footprints. So now all we need is a suspect with the same stuff on their shoes," said Romero. "And right now that's a real long shot."

"When I checked out the suspect's houses I didn't notice a pair of grubby boots in any of the closets at the compound. If there were, I imagine one of the wives probably scrubbed them up spic and span," McCabe said.

On the trek back to their vehicle, McCabe paused to pull a burr stuck to the cuff of his jeans. As he knelt on the hard ground, he looked up at the detective. "You okay, Rick?"

Romero's brow furrowed. "Nah, my brain's been idling in overdrive on this case," he said.

"I know what you mean. It's a little early to come to any serious conclusions, you think?" McCabe said.

"This case is making me a little uncomfortable. On the one hand, if Hodge committed the crime, he will have to go through the courts to determine his guilt or innocence. On the other hand, this man is technically my father-in-law, even though we haven't formally discussed this. I'm a little confused as to what my obligations are here," Romero said.

"I would imagine Jemimah is going through the same confusion. Bottom line, our job is to gather enough evidence to present to the DA. We don't make the decisions as to guilt or innocence," McCabe said.

Romero patted him on the shoulder. "Leave it to you to throw in some clarity. You're right, of course."

They reached the vehicle just as the rain started to pour. By the time they turned onto the highway, the windshield wipers were going twenty miles an hour.

Chapter Twenty-Three

JEMIMAH WAS PENSIVE as she dressed for work. For the second time she pored through her closet, then chose a fitted blue jacket, a white knit tee and dark jeans. A color-blocked silk scarf looped around her neck. On her way into work that morning, she stopped at the substation to obtain copies of Detective Romero's case notes.

He kissed her softly and handed her the file and motioned her to sit. "Let me remind you again, my dear Doctor Hodge, that you have the option to assign the interviews to someone else. I can probably get one of the rookies to do this. Might save you a lot of grief."

She shrugged. "I know, but Sheriff Medrano's been complaining about being understaffed, and I'm sure his budget doesn't have enough flexibility to bring in someone else, particularly someone qualified. It's not just about taking interviews; Katie could do that. It's about being able to profile the witness, using the skills I've developed in my practice over the years."

"Nobody's better at it than you are."

She grinned at him. "You're prejudiced, and you have to say that, you're my husband."

"Yes, but I was a great admirer of your unique skills long before we married."

She tilted her head back and laughed. "I'm not sure we're talking about the same skills." She checked her phone for the time. "I need to run. I'm anxious to look through the file and get these interviews developed. It's going to be my first project under my new title."

Romero stood to walk her to the door. Jemimah kissed him on the cheek. Out in the parking lot he waited while she buckled up. She threw him a kiss and waved as she pulled out.

Jemimah cranked up the volume on the FM station as she made her way through the orange barrels spread across the centerline of the highway. She was determined that the recent events had fallen into her lap for a reason and she was not going to let anything affect her performance. Over the years she had wondered how she would react if she ever came face to face with someone from her past. She was about to find out, and she knew it was going to be a good day when one of her favorite Beatles' songs came on the air as she rounded the turn on San Francisco Street. "Let it be".

Katie Gonzales, her longtime assistant, was waiting at the door when Jemimah strolled up the hallway toward her office. Katie ran toward her and gave her a big bear hug. "Oh, my God, it is so nice to see you again, Doc! Or should I say Mrs. Doc," she laughed, "or Mrs. Detective."

Jemimah returned the embrace, a grin on her face. "Same here, Katie. I'm so glad Sheriff Medrano decided to give us both back our old jobs and that his office was able to contact you before you went off to greener pastures," she said.

"Yes, that was really cool, accompanied by a nice little raise, based of course on your promotion. I wasn't too excited about being transferred to the DA's office, so it worked out for me," Katie said. "I heard about the Sheriff causing you guys to postpone your honeymoon. That sucks."

"Yes, it does," Jemimah said. "But things are working out."

Katie had worked part-time for Jemimah as her assistant

through a number of cases in the previous years. Her four-foot-eleven frame consisted of a curvy body, short brown hair and a bubbly personality. Dark brown eyes and long lashes completed the picture. She was also a serial dater, and tended to pop in and out of relationships.

Jemimah slipped her purse into a drawer and placed the manila folder on the desk. "This is our first official case, Katie, and you're not going to believe what it's all about."

"Sounds like we're going to need some coffee. Hold that thought," Katie said. She slipped into the kitchen and prepared a tray with two coffees, cream and sugar and threw in a couple of pastries for good measure. She set them out neatly on the conference room table. "Okay, we're all set."

Between bites of a cheese Danish, Jemimah related the entire scenario that Detective Romero had presented the evening before. A couple of times she felt a knot building in her throat, but worked through it. When she was finished, her eyes were misted. "Darned allergies," she said.

Katie slid the tissue box toward Jemimah. "Wow, Doc. This is definitely a Kleenex moment. I just have one dumb question."

"Shoot," Jemimah said.

"Does this mean that those four women you mentioned are all your mothers?"

"If I followed the religion, they would be, I guess. But I got away from that when I was in my late teens, and I've never looked back. Only one of them is my birth mother."

"So these are Mormons?" Katie said.

"No, technically they are referred to as FLDS. Fundamentalist Latter Day Saints, which I understand is a radical offshoot that pulled away from the teachings of the Mormon Church years ago. I'm sure you've read something in the paper about them?"

"Oh yeah, that fellow Warren Jeffs who was jailed last year for marrying off some fourteen year old girls to a bunch of old men?"

"Yes, that would be it. For the most part, they are a

polygamist sect who believe in all manner of things, led by this individual. His followers go right along with everything he says, believing that he is some kind of prophet, even as he sits in prison," Jemimah said.

"Do you think your father was involved in any of that?"

Jemimah sat back in her chair. "I can't say for sure, but knowing him as I did, he was pretty stubborn and I doubt if someone like Jeffs would be able to make him follow the rules, at least not for the long haul. Even then, he seemed to be fairly set in his own way."

"How are you going to feel about conducting these interviews, Doc, as I assume we are going to be doing?" Katie asked.

"We are. At first I was concerned there might be a conflict. Even though I'm technically related to not only the suspect, but also only two of the wives, the District Attorney cleared it. He determined that my interviews would not be of a personal nature. I had nothing to gain from them and the fact that I've had no contact with these individuals for over twenty years played heavily on his decision. Because of that, I'm pretty sure I can be objective. After all, we're just going to interview as many witnesses as there are in this case and add those to the investigation." Hearing these words come out of her mouth, Jemimah felt more comfortable about the situation.

"One last question. Are you required to interview your father, the prime suspect in this case?" Katie said.

"Fortunately, no. When he was arrested, he immediately requested an attorney, who put the kiebash on any interviews. The only thing they have is Detective Romero's arrest notes," Jemimah said. "I will say one thing, though. The events of this past week have pushed my stress level way up. When all is said and done, I'm going to have to call in the big guns...my therapist, Dr. Cade."

Katie cleared the table and took the empty cups into the kitchen. "I'd be sitting in his office right about now. You're a lot braver about this than I would be, Doc. I admire that."

Jemimah laughed. "Don't go admiring prematurely. We are going to see exactly how this will play out and it could go either way. Now, let's get our heads together, review the file, and make up a list of pertinent questions. I made the initial contact and they'll be coming in day after tomorrow at ten."

Katie had a concerned look on her face. "Jeez, Doc, are you sure you're up for this? All of them together? Wouldn't it be easier to schedule them one at a time?"

Jemimah shrugged. "This is all part of my job, Katie. When Sheriff Medrano assigned this case to me, I gave him my word that I would not let personal feelings enter into my assessment of the witnesses, and I fully intend to do that, so chop chop."

Katie laughed. "Ha ha, you mean *andale*, don't you? Hurry up!"

Chapter Twenty-Four

JEMIMAH HAD ONE more person she wanted to add to her interview list. Maybe not so much wanted as knew it was necessary to get some facts straight in her own mind. That would be Byron Mills, and she would have to bite her tongue on this one.

Mills was a throwback to the days Jemimah lived with her parents in Utah about the time her father decided to join the FLDS group. Over the years, Mills had made a number of attempts to contact Jemimah, and she avoided him like the plague he was. She ran into him unexpectedly on two occasions, once at the Barkin' Ball fundraiser for the animal shelter where Tim McCabe rescued her from his clutches, and then again when he dropped by her office. At that time, she was not willing to see him and threatened to have Security escort him out. Mills bolted out of her office with disgust on his face, sputtering expletives as he left. Jemimah wasn't sure about seeing him again, but decided she needed to set her personal feelings aside.

On her laptop, she Googled the Santa Fe white pages and found a phone number for Mills. She tapped the number into her cell phone and was about to hang up when he answered on the fourth ring.

"Mr. Mills, this is Jemimah Hodge. Do you have a moment?" she said, her hand gripping the arm of the chair.

She could almost envision the syrup dripping from his mouth. "Jemimah, how nice to hear from you. A voice from the past, as they say. Is this a social call or are you acting in the capacity of your position with the Sheriff's Office. You're still employed there, I assume."

"Yes, I am. Let me cut to the chase, Byron. I'm sure you're aware that Jason Hodge has been arrested," she said.

"I am. In fact, I've been out to see him several times. Poor fellow. The judge threw him in jail without setting bail, but I understand he's hired a good attorney."

"I'm not calling for an update," Jemimah said. "I would like to ask if you could come in for an interview. I have a number of questions that you might be able to shed some light on."

"Are you asking me to be a witness against your father?"

"No, of course not. Let me clarify. Part of my job is to interview witnesses to determine what they know about a particular case. Sometimes the information gathered can be used in court, but generally is used to form a profile of suspects. In your case, I'm just looking for information to fill in some of the blanks about Jason Hodge and his life. It isn't to either help or hinder, just for me to become more familiar with what we're dealing with," she said, annoyed at herself for talking in circles. What was it about this man that caused her to lose her composure?

Mills was silent for a moment. "Hmmm, I think we both know that you've treated me with great disrespect and hostility in the past, particularly since my only aim was to put you in touch with your parents, who had not heard from you for quite a long time. I'm not sure I want to expose myself to that kind of treatment again," he said.

As distasteful as the prospect was of being in the same room with this detestable person, Jemimah swallowed her pride. "I can assure you, Byron, that my primary purpose is to compile witness information in this case, and the only way I can do that is to get a full picture of the accused. I believe you can fill in some of the gaps. However, if this is something that might cause you discomfort, I can look elsewhere," she said. "Nothing has changed my unwillingness to spend time with you taking a trip down memory lane."

After hemming and hawing for what seemed like an eternity, Mills agreed to come by her office the following day. Jemimah thanked him and hung up the phone. She stared out the window at the traffic below. She could feel her heart skip a beat. *I hope I'm not biting off more than I can handle.*

Chapter Twenty-Five

JEMIMAH'S FIRST SCHEDULED interview that morning was that of Eliza Simpson, the fiancée of the victim. As Katie explained while Jemimah settled in, the woman was only going to be in Santa Fe long enough to make funeral arrangements and have the body transported back to Utah for burial, so she had taken the liberty of having her come in. Jemimah was looking through the paperwork in the file and scribbled some final notes when Katie tapped on the door.

"Your appointment has arrived, shall I show her in?" she said.

Jemimah nodded. "Yes, let's do this."

Katie directed the woman in and introduced her to Jemimah.

Jemimah glanced up at the woman with curly brown hair and deep brown eyes standing before her, casually dressed, but fashionable in a green knitted top with white pedal-pushers and cork sandals.

"Miss Simpson, thank you for agreeing to come in. First, let me say how sorry I am for the loss of your fiancé. The news must have come as a great shock," Jemimah said.

Eliza Simpson lowered herself into the chair near the desk.

"Yes, it did, thank you."

Jemimah pushed the box of tissues across the desk. "Part of my job is to try to develop information about victims and witnesses to a particular crime. I hope you don't mind if I ask you a few questions which might help me do this. My assistant mentioned you will be leaving Santa Fe soon, so I'm hoping this won't delay your travel," she said.

Eliza pulled a tissue from the box. "No, I'm just waiting for the release of the body so I can move on."

Jemimah noticed the look of anguish on her face. "I'll try to be brief. Do you have someone back home who can provide some emotional support? I'm sure the coming weeks will be difficult for you," she said.

Eliza thought for a moment. "I do have Bishop Kimball, and oh, yes, Dr. Blake Parker. I can always call him if I need to, but I think I can handle this situation," she said, with more emphasis than Jemimah thought was necessary, but chocked it off to her fragile state of mind.

"Very well," Jemimah said. "I understand that you spoke with Detective Romero a few days ago, so I apologize if I repeat something you might have already covered. First of all, can you tell me something about your relationship with Mr. Tanner? How long had you known him?"

Eliza wadded up the tissue in her hand. "We met several years ago at a religious seminar. I was speaking on the psychology of religion and he spoke about the importance of missions. He was recently divorced and I was widowed. We became friends since we were on the same committee. Eventually we started dating, and we became engaged about six months ago. We were waiting for the Church to finalize his annulment before we could set a date," she said.

Noticing the quizzical look on Jemimah's face, she waved her hand. "A divorce in the Mormon Church is not like a regular divorce," she explained. "As I understand it, his marriage has to be annulled, a temple sealing cancellation, if you will. Then that person can be assured of his status in eternal life. I know that sounds confusing, but that's the best I can do."

Jemimah nodded. "I have limited knowledge about Mormon life, but that sounds clear enough. Can you tell me what kind of person Mr. Tanner was?"

Eliza clasped her hands in her lap. "Oh, he was a kind and thoughtful man, all the nice things you can say about a human being and really mean them. He was extremely religious and dedicated to the Mormon Church, and was being considered for placement in an upper level of the hierarchy." She lowered her head, a tear rolling down her cheek.

Jemimah waited. "I'm sure this must be painful, but these questions will help us in solving the case. Please bear with me. Did you hear from him after he left on this trip to Albuquerque?" she said.

"Yes, he texted me when he arrived at the airport there to say he had rented a car and was headed to the hotel, but we had agreed he wouldn't be calling regularly as he was going to be very busy. These meetings generally involve hands-on participation with teens and go on all day and sometimes late into the evening."

"At what point did you become concerned?" Jemimah said.

"I knew he was expected to fly back that weekend and he had promised to call so I could pick him up at the airport, but I hadn't heard from him. So I waited all night by the phone. I tried his cell repeatedly, but there was no answer. Then I called Bishop Kimball and he assured me Lawrence probably overslept and missed his flight, not only because he was prone to do so, but because of the altitude in this area," she said, fanning her face. "I've noticed it myself. The bishop also said that Lawrence might have mentioned in passing that since he was so close to Santa Fe, he was going there to look around."

"What did you do then?" Jemimah asked.

She sighed. "I did some searches on the Internet and got a list of hotels in Santa Fe and after calling a number of them, I found him registered at the Holiday Inn. He had been there since two days before and was scheduled to check out the next day. The clerk tried the room and there was no answer."

"What time of day was that?" Jemimah said.

"I believe it was about seven-thirty in the evening. It wasn't quite dark in Provo," she said.

"So that would be an hour earlier than Mountain Time?"

"Yes, I guess so. So I was up most of the night, kept trying his phone, and I even called the local hospital to see if maybe he had fallen sick, but there was no trace of him."

"Did he have any physical disabilities or health problems that you know of?" Jemimah said.

She fiddled with a hairpin. "He had a mild case of diabetes, but it was kept under control by diet and medication. Nothing serious, he just had to watch what he ate."

"What did you do next?," Jemimah asked.

"The next morning I called the hotel again and asked them if they would please go to his room, and they did. I waited while the desk clerk sent someone up there, and then he told me they found nothing amiss, his luggage was still in the room, along with toiletries still on the vanity. The clerk assured me that tourists come to Santa Fe and then get all caught up in so many things to do and lose track of time," she said.

"Did you check back with the hotel again?" Jemimah said.

"Yes, by that evening I had really started to get worried, because when housekeeping went in the room to clean up, everything was still the same. The bed had not been slept in," she said, reaching for the tissue box again.

Jemimah walked to the kitchen, retrieved a bottle of water and handed it to Eliza, waiting while she regained her composure. "Do you know what reason he would have to be in Santa Fe, since it was not part of his itinerary?"

"Lawrence had always been interested in Pueblo Indian pottery and he probably took this opportunity to explore, being that he was so close to Santa Fe. Knowing him, I know he wouldn't pass up a junket into some of the pueblos around the area. I don't recall him mentioning that, but even if he had, I wouldn't have minded because I was busy preparing for an upcoming church event and had too much to do to concern myself. As it was, it was going to be inconvenient for me to pick him up that evening when he was supposed to arrive, but I felt it was my duty," she said.

Jemimah placed a few checkmarks on her tablet. "Let's change the subject here. What can you tell me about his ex-wife, Brigid Tanner, I believe is her name?"

Eliza inhaled deeply and adjusted her position in the chair. Jemimah wasn't prepared for what she would hear next.

Chapter Twenty-Six

Eliza Simpson's forehead suddenly had deep furrows and her eyebrows arched noticeably. "Quite frankly, the woman was a real bitch."

In a five minute monologue, she related to Jemimah that toward the end of the marriage Lawrence's wife had become involved with an FLDS leader and that her fiancé had locked horns with him in the past.

"Was this before the divorce or after?" Jemimah said.

"I think it was right before he filed, or maybe that was the reason he filed. He didn't like to talk about it," she said.

"When you say locked horns, did they have an altercation?"

"More of a run-in, I would say. Provo has a small town mentality, everyone knows each other, so you can't help running into people whether you intend to or not," she said.

"So this was an unintentional incident. They just happened to be in the same place at the same time," Jemimah said.

She nodded. "You could say that. Lawrence had always expressed the opinion that this man had coerced and manipulated his wife into joining his polygamist sect, and I believe he took the opportunity to accuse him of such, having held it inside for so long," Eliza said.

Jemimah was silent for a moment. "Do you know this man's name?"

"I believe it was Jason Hodge, the fellow they've arrested for the murder. I saw his picture in the newspaper, and that was him, I'm sure."

"What other impression did you have of Brigid Tanner?" Jemimah said.

"I understand she had been excommunicated from the religion and it didn't seem to bother her a bit," she said.

"And did that bother your fiancé?"

"He said he should have known that she would never fit in. She was too gregarious, too in-your-face, as they say, and apparently very self-centered. I personally think it should have been good riddance."

Jemimah noticed the subtle clench of Eliza's fist as she spoke. "In other words, she didn't know her place?"

She stuck out her chin. "It appears that was the case. She was not a typical Mormon wife, if you know what I mean. She ended the relationship with Lawrence sometime after meeting Hodge. My fiancé didn't like how she flaunted that relationship before him. It was as though she was taunting him with it. Lawrence was a moral and upright man, and he tried to ignore it, but he was human," she said.

Jemimah checked the time remaining on the recorder. "One more question before we conclude our interview. Do you have an opinion as to who would have wanted to hurt your fiancé, anyone who had something against him?"

Eliza Simpson craned her neck and leaned forward. "Nobody other than the person who's been arrested. I hope that man burns in hell for what he did. Because of him, my life has come to a standstill."

"I am sure justice will be served in whatever manner is necessary," Jemimah said. She thanked the witness for her time and handed her one of her cards.

Chapter Twenty-Seven

BYRON MILLS WAS a tall, wiry man with a prominent nose and cold, dark eyes. His heavily pomaded hair was a deep chocolate brown, obviously dyed, the white roots growing out on the crown of his head. As was his manner, he was dressed in a snappy, tailored suit with a pink shirt, striped bowtie and polished designer shoes. As he strutted into Jemimah's office suite, he pulled the Armani sunglasses from his face with an exaggerated flourish.

Katie came out of her cubbyhole and greeted him. "Mr. Mills, Dr. Hodge is in the middle of a conference call and will be with you shortly. Can I get you some coffee?" She could feel his eyes traveling around her body.

Mills declined the offer, but continued to stare in her direction. "Make yourself comfortable," Katie said, and stepped into Jemimah's office, where she waited for her to conclude the phone call.

Jemimah placed her hand over the receiver and motioned for her to come in. "I take it my next appointment is here?"

Katie rolled her eyes and moved her body in an exaggerated shiver. "Jeez, the guy gives me the creeps. What rock did he slide out from under?"

Jemimah nodded in agreement. "Show him in, Katie. The sooner I get this over with, the better."

She ended her conversation as Mills entered her office and stood before her desk, leaning forward to Jemimah's cheek. She stuck out her hand.

"Byron, thank you for coming." She motioned toward the chair next to her desk. "Please, have a seat."

He tapped the palms of his hands together like a child receiving a treat. "At long last I get to sit down with you and talk, Jemimah. I'm looking forward to catching up," he said.

Jemimah pointed the palm of her hand toward him. "At a different time, perhaps. In this instance, let's just set aside the formalities and get started. Do you mind if I record our meeting so I won't have to write down everything you say?"

Mills stiffened his shoulders at the rebuff and didn't answer for a second. "I guess that should be all right. *I'm* not the one under investigation here."

Jemimah forced a smile. "No, you are not. I'm not asking you to reveal any deep dark secrets here. I'm just asking you to help clear up a few things for me."

She flicked the recorder on and repeated the date and time and the name and purpose of the interview. "Byron, can you bring me up to date on what's been going on in the Hodge community since I left Utah some years ago? I'm not interested in details, just generalities."

"Well, your father, Hodge, as you wish to refer to him, pulled away from the Mormon Church, joined the FLDS, and later left that group some years after that. He decided to take his wives and children and go off on his own," he said.

"Was there any particular reason?" Jemimah said. "When I ran away, he had enmeshed himself into the FLDS and had two wives with another candidate looming in the background."

He waved his hand. "That one didn't work out, but another one, Hannah Rebecca, came in about a year after you left. To answer your question, he pulled away because although he still believed in polygamy, he didn't believe in that leader's precepts.

No one was going to choose his wives for him, particularly one that promulgated marriage to girls barely out of puberty."

Jemimah was glad to hear that, score one for Jason Hodge. She considered it a good point, since one of the reasons she ran away was because she was determined not to be married off herself. She didn't stick around long enough for him to change his mind.

Mills continued. "He also objected to having teenaged boys shipped out on what the group called repentance missions, solely designed to keep them from developing romantic relationships with girls their age. At one time, Hodge had his own group of devoted followers and it was hoped he would become their leader, but then the FLDS became the target of investigations from all corners of the surrounding states, widespread allegations of organized welfare fraud and sexual abuse. He wouldn't stand behind the leader's son, who had taken over after his father's arrest. Hodge became a very unpopular man within the FLDS community for his outspoken nature, so in essence, he gathered up his wives and children and moved them to Colorado, where because of anti-polygamy laws, the group was harassed on a regular basis."

"How did they land up here in New Mexico?" Jemimah said.

Mills puffed up his chest. "Well, that was part of my doing. As you know, I am a realtor. I found them a piece of land in a remote community southeast of Santa Fe. Pretty close to your place, if I might add, but at the time I didn't know where you lived, and neither did they. This was about a hundred acres of ranchland and forest land abutting the Ortiz Mountain Range. Used to be some kind of a new age religious retreat, so I figured it would be perfect for them with a few modifications. Out of the way, and such."

Jemimah offered him a bottle of water and walked to the kitchen, placing one on the desk for herself and handing him the other. Mills unscrewed the cap and took a big gulp, then set the bottle down.

"Thank you," he said. "Where was I? So in the first six months they did a little remodeling, splitting up the compound so that there were four equal houses. It's a nice place, you should go out there sometime," he said.

"Out of curiosity, where are the children? I haven't heard any mention of them being housed at the complex," Jemimah said.

"Far as I know, most of the children from this family group are all grown up. Might be one or two teenagers that they left back in Utah with relatives until they settled in," he said, "but most of them have gone on to college or to live their own lives. And, of course," he added, "these women are no longer of childbearing age, so there haven't been new additions for some time. I understand the newest wife isn't interested in having children, I might add, a fact your father was probably relieved to hear."

Jemimah recalled her only full sibling, a brother, would now be about her age, but didn't inquire as to his whereabouts. She didn't have to, as Mills read her mind and volunteered the information.

"Your younger brother moved away from Utah as soon as he hit eighteen. I don't think he's kept in touch with the family either. Last I heard he had joined the Army and was permanently stationed overseas somewhere, Afghanistan or the like." Mills stifled a yawn and pulled a pocket watch from his trousers. "Anything else you need to know?"

Jemimah tapped the off button on the recorder. "I think we've covered it all." She pushed her chair back and stood. "Byron, I want to thank you for taking time to do this. It's been a great help."

"Anything I can do to help Hodge out. You know, Jemimah, he is not the kind of man that would do harm to anyone. I know they found a weapon in one of the houses, but I can assure you that he has never believed in guns and probably never owned one," he said.

"Yes, I'm sure you know him better than most. I'll add that

to my notes." She motioned to the door. "I think you can find your way out."

Jemimah spent the remainder of the day putting her notes in some semblance of order. Before she left for the day, Katie handed her a transcribed copy of the conversation she had earlier with Byron Mills, which she slid into the file.

By the time five o'clock roared around, she knew more about her family's FLDS life than when she left over twenty years before. She wasn't too surprised to hear how things had turned out.

Chapter Twenty-Eight

K ATIE WAS ALREADY sitting at her desk when Jemimah arrived at her office that Friday morning. Leaning over her was a handsome young man with an engaging smile, somewhere in his mid-twenties, dressed in a muscle-hugging dark shirt and trousers. Jemimah was well aware that Katie was a serial dater and seemed to attract a wide variety of suitors wherever she went. They both looked up as she entered the room.

The obviously embarrassed young man stood. "Morning, Doc", Katie said. "This is David, he works downstairs in Security."

David reached out to shake her hand. "Doctor Hodge, yes, I've seen your name on our roster. It's nice to meet you."

Jemimah smiled, about to say something as Katie stood and shooed him out. She reached up on tiptoes and whispered in his ear before he reached the door.

She looked at Jemimah. "Just a friend, FYI."

"You have a number of good-looking friends. Very nice. How can you not be serious about this one? He's gorgeous," Jemimah said.

Katie laughed. "Still playing the field, thank you. I'll be the first to know when I find Mister Wonderful."

"He looked pretty wonderful to me," Jemimah chuckled.

"On another note, Doc, are you ready to face the day? Your appointments start in about an hour," Katie said.

Jemimah dumped her purse and satchel on the floor under the desk. "Gives me time to bolster my courage with caffeine." She strolled over to the kitchen to look for her favorite mug. She didn't want to admit it, but she could feel a lump forming in her throat. She infused a stream of cream into a large cup of coffee and retreated to her desk to try to relax.

"Katie, in order to guarantee there is no future question of wrongdoing on my part by interviewing someone I might be acquainted with, I need for you to be present in the room and in charge of recording the conversations," she said.

"That's a good idea, Doc. No point in leaving yourself open to criticism if you can avoid it," Katie said.

The four women arrived promptly at ten. Katie escorted them into the waiting room and offered them water or coffee, which they collectively declined. Jemimah took a deep breath and came out of her office to introduce herself. There was no question which one of them was her mother, Clara, and which one was Kathryn, the second wife. The other two she didn't recognize at all. She hesitated as she reached out stiffly to embrace her mother and Kathryn, and shook hands with the other two. Each was dressed in casual clothes, light lipstick and makeup, and neatly coiffed hair, unlike the dull prairie dresses and French twist updo portrayed in the media.

Jemimah turned to face the women. "I need to make a blanket statement here, due to the particular circumstances which we have. Since there are four of you, I will be asking a similar set of questions to each. I would request that you answer those questions as truthfully as you can, particularly those that relate to your whereabouts for the seventy-two hours preceding the crime in question."

The women looked at each other.

Jemimah continued. "I know that on the surface this

appears somewhat daunting, but as Detective Romero probably mentioned, the subject of these conversations will not be shared with one another, so feel free to be as specific as you wish. In the overall picture, you are all suspects even though the Sheriff has chosen to focus on Jason Hodge, the last person they believe who saw the victim alive. Are you all okay with that?"

The wives nodded in unison.

"And let me add that my aim here is to amass information through these interviews that can give law enforcement some idea of what has occurred on the sidelines. We are not pointing the finger at anyone. Miss Gonzales, my assistant, will be present during our interviews." She turned to Katie. "Let's get started. Would you please escort Kathryn to my office?"

Katie did as she was instructed, then took her place in the chair to the left of Jemimah and set the recorder on the desk in front of her. Kathryn sat across from Jemimah.

Kathryn was the second wife whom Jemimah met when she was around eleven or so. She was dark haired and petite, and hadn't changed much since Jemimah had last seen her so many years before. She was dressed in white trousers and a striped cardigan, leather clogs and a pink scarf. She started to tell Jemimah how nice it was to see her after all this time, and the difficult circumstances that had brought them together.

Jemimah forced a smile. "Yes, I understand, but since there are four of you, we need to get under way."

She spent the next hour asking questions of Kathryn, and then moved on to Hannah Rebecca, the third wife in the group. She was younger than the other two by a few years. She was about as tall as Jemimah and had brownish hair pulled back in a ponytail. She was dressed in dark jeans and an oversized red shirt. The questions Jemimah asked varied only slightly in content, as did the responses. Like the others, Hannah described their husband as charismatic, kind, generous, a strong and fair leader.

When the interview came to a close, Jemimah thanked her

and Katie escorted her back to the waiting room.

The next person in line was Brigid Tanner, who was the ex-wife of the victim and the fourth wife in the group. She walked briskly into Jemimah's office and took a seat. Her long brown hair was braided into two pigtails. Abundant lashes lined searching green eyes that appeared to take in everything around her. She had perfect eyebrows and perfect teeth, and a bubbly personality. Wisps of stray hair were neatly pinned under a colorful barrette. Jemimah had to admit she was a very attractive woman and found it hard to understand how she could be attracted to an aging man with three other wives. She suspected Brigid was much younger than her father and the other wives and wondered what they really thought of her.

"Brigid, your circumstances appear to be different than those of your sister wives. You are related to both the person who has been arrested and to the victim. Let me assure you, as I have the others, that any statement you make will not be shared with the other wives, so I would encourage you to be as open as possible. Agree?" Jemimah said.

"Of course, I have nothing to hide. Ask away," she said, adding that the sister wives had only known her since Hodge introduced her into the fold.

Katie flipped the switch on the recorder, indicating the date, time and identification of the witness. Jemimah asked her first question. "Brigid, were you already divorced from Lawrence Tanner when you met Jason Hodge?"

"Yes, or shortly before. I don't remember exactly. Lawrence and I were at the farmer's market standing in front of one of the vendors, and Hodge sidled up beside us and reached for a bundle of carrots almost knocking the basket out of my hand. Of course he tipped his head and apologized. It may sound like a fairy tale, but our eyes met and I felt something very magnetic. The relationship between my husband and myself had been eroding for some time, but it was never my intent to get involved with another man. Eventually Lawrence filed for divorce and a few weeks later I ran into Jason again. He took me to lunch and we met several times after that," she said.

"Was your ex-husband aware of your involvement?" Jemimah asked.

"Eventually. He once saw us in a local diner and put two and two together."

"How did Tanner react?" said Jemimah.

"They had a minor confrontation, with Lawrence accusing Jason of manipulating me and trying to coerce me into becoming one of his wives," she said. "I could sense an intense animosity in his manner, as he tried to bully Jason into a fight."

"And was Mr. Hodge doing that, manipulating you?"

She waved her hand. "No, of course not. We were infatuated with each other, and typical of bullies, my ex-husband made a few veiled threats. He knew nothing about Jason and more than likely wouldn't be able to find anything out. He was angry because I wouldn't reconcile with him and accused me of being under the influence of this man, as if he was some kind of Svengali. I was in the relationship of my own volition. I wasn't manipulated into it."

"On the next occasion that they ran into each other, what happened?" Jemimah said.

"They had a heated discussion, maybe not a confrontation, as we were in a public place. My ex-husband told Jason he should be ashamed of himself for enticing a perfectly innocent woman, me, into his concubine," Brigid said.

"And what was Jason Hodge's reaction to that?"

"He told my ex that we had a perfectly legitimate relationship, and it should be none of his concern what I did since I was no longer in the marriage. Then Lawrence muttered something and turned and stomped off. I've never seen him so angry."

"If I might ask, why did you divorce him in the first place?"

Brigid tugged nervously at her earlobe. "There were a number of reasons, but I guess the main issue was that for several years my heart hadn't been into the religion. I was a convert to Mormonism, otherwise we couldn't have married. I was required to behave in a certain way, I never felt like myself, that I was playing a part no matter how hard I tried. I began to resent my subservient role and after a while I realized I didn't want to live that way any longer. Lawrence was oblivious. He was more interested in preserving the illusion than of facing the truth."

"Do you know how Jason Hodge felt about your ex-husband?" Jemimah said.

"We didn't talk much about that, but deep down I was always worried they would butt heads someday. My ex-husband pushed hard for me to see the error of my ways and reconcile with him. Jason said I was his now and there was no way he would ever let me go," Brigid said.

"So you had two men, each pulling you in opposite directions?" Jemimah said.

She blushed. "It would seem so, but I had already made up my mind to stay where I was."

"Did you believe that Jason Hodge would at some point leave his other wives for you?"

She shrugged. "Well, he promised, and I knew him to be a man of his word."

"Did he ever express concern that you might return to your ex-husband if he went back on his word?"

"We never discussed it on those terms. I made it abundantly clear that I wasn't comfortable sharing him with three other women, so something better happen soon," she said. "I was aware he had three other wives, and after many discussions about joining the group, I realized it was something I didn't think I could do. He wanted me and I wanted him, but I wasn't willing to share him. We found ourselves in a dilemma, to say the least."

"How long before you consented to become the fourth woman in the group?" Jemimah said.

"Jason convinced me to join the other sister wives for the interim, and that as soon as he could see his way clear, we would go off together. He would have to file for divorce from his first wife and then leave all three of them, but first he wanted to make sure everything was taken care of and there were no loose ends."

"How old are you, if I may ask?" Jemimah said.

"Twenty-nine."

Jemimah couldn't help herself from asking the next question. It was more for her own information than for the interview. "You're talking about a sixty-some year old man. That's quite an age difference."

Brigid clasped her hands to her chest. "Oh, but Jason is so much younger in spirit. It was as though he had a new found reason to live and enjoy life. He'd had so many years of dealing with three wives and eighteen children, never a moment to himself. Whatever other reasons he had, I can't say, but he expressed a deep love for me and I for him."

Jemimah was tempted to say that this was the life he had chosen for himself and his wives, but she knew it was all none of her concern. She continued. "So when were you introduced to the other wives?"

A small grin crossed her face. "It took a while for him to convince me, but I finally gave in. He had explained how it worked and promised me it wouldn't be long before we were together, so I agreed."

Jemimah glanced up at the clock on the wall and motioned for Katie to stop recording. "Brigid, would there be a problem with continuing our interview this afternoon? I'm sure you ladies would like to take a break and have lunch?"

She pulled herself up. "Yes, I'm sure my sister wives would agree that would be a good idea. We had a light breakfast and hardly ever have a chance to explore the downtown area. This would be a perfect opportunity."

Katie walked Brigid out to the waiting room. After the women departed from the office, she returned to Jemimah's office. She sat in the easy chair and smoothed her hair over her ears. "Wow, Dr. Hodge, that was intense. How are you holding up?"

"As best I can. But we've barely skimmed over the surface. I'm sure this afternoon will be just as enlightening." She stood up and stretched her arms above her head. "I'm starving, let's get some lunch."

Chapter Twenty-Nine

After a quick take-out lunch of chicken quesadillas from the Plaza Café downstairs, Jemimah sat at her desk with Katie and glossed over her notes.

"You know, Katie, this interview with the fourth wife is taking a lot longer than I imagined. I think I'll start the afternoon with the first wife, and then finish up with Brigid," she said.

Katie arched her eyebrows. "Any particular reason, Doc? That's the one I was worried would be the most difficult for you, being as she's your birth mother and all," she said.

Jemimah sighed. "I know, but I need to get it over with. I'm not sure she can add much to the investigation. Brigid, on the other hand, could conceivably hold a lot more information that might be pertinent to the case, so I need to focus a little more on that."

Katie agreed. "You're the boss. I'll be sitting at your side for moral support. If the pressure starts to get to you, give me a signal and I'll make an excuse for a break."

"They should be returning soon. I told them we would resume at one-thirty," Jemimah said. She reached in the drawer for her purse and walked down the hall to the ladies' room and touched up her lipstick. She wondered if her level of anxiety would be apparent when she was face to face with her birth mother. She didn't have long to wait. As she dried her hands and started back down the hall, the women had just entered her office.

Katie stood in the reception room. "Ladies, we found it necessary to change up the order a bit. Clara will go next and then we'll finish up with Brigid. I hope that's all right."

The women nodded. Katie directed Clara Hodge to Jemimah's office and pulled out the chair in front of the desk for her and sat down in her morning space.

Clara smiled uneasily. "Hello, again, Jemimah," she said. "It's good to see that you've come a long way since the last time we were together."

Jemimah looked into the gray-green eyes of the woman she had only known for the first sixteen years of her life. It was unsettling to momentarily return to the past and picture the vibrant woman with long brown hair who held her hand as they walked to the public school near their home in Hildale; the woman who laughed freely, prepared meals with gusto, and enjoyed visiting with other mothers as they waited for the dismissal bell to ring at the school. It was all Jemimah could do to keep her emotions in check. She inhaled deeply.

Jemimah nodded. "Yes, it has been a long time. Unfortunately these are circumstances which neither of us could have predicted." She paused. "If you don't mind, we should dispense with formalities and focus on the situation before us," she said.

"Yes, of course. I'm hopeful there will be a less stressful time when we can sit down and talk, if you're open to that," Clara said.

"I can't promise anything, but I will say that at this moment in time, my attention has to be concentrated on gathering information that will help move this case along. I'm sorry for the predicament you women find yourselves in, but from my experience, justice will always prevail in these matters, cliché as it may sound," she said.

Clara Hodge clasped her hands in her lap. "Very well, what do you need to know?"

Jemimah spent a little over forty-five minutes asking questions about where Jason Hodge was or had been in the two days preceding the finding of the victim's body. Clara Hodge's answers were fairly consistent with those of the other women. Her husband had exhibited no noticeable shifts in his typically predictable behavior. He was working on finishing off the details in each of the houses, the barn and the studio. He was neither anxious nor stressed and his demeanor had not visibly changed in any way that she could see.

"As you know, Jemimah, your father and I have been together for over forty years. I'm fairly certain I would be able to recognize even the slightest shift in his behavior," she said.

"I have a more personal question to ask, and I hope it doesn't offend you. What did you feel when your husband informed you and the other wives that he was bringing Brigid Tanner into the fold?" Jemimah said.

Clara Hodge's eyes widened. "I know you said our comments and opinions wouldn't be shared, but that's a difficult question."

"Take all the time you need," Jemimah said.

Katie walked to the kitchen and returned with a bottle of water. Clara thanked her and took a long sip. She inhaled deeply. "To be quite honest, it took me by surprise. All these years we've worked toward getting all the children educated and prepared for adult life, and to learn one day that Jason was interested in yet another woman was very depressing, to say the least."

"How did you learn of the proposal?" Jemimah said.

"I suspected their relationship started before any of us knew about it. They were meeting in secret while her divorce was finalized. The only reason we became aware of this was because one of the older children had seen them together more than once," she said.

Jemimah could see moisture forming around her eyes. "Did you discuss your feelings with him?"

"I think I just expressed anger and frustration, but as it had been in the past, my opinion didn't matter. He had made up his mind, and that was that," she said. "Once Brigid was integrated into the group, I can honestly say I didn't change my position one bit, but he made it abundantly clear to all of us that he expected her to be treated with the same respect we felt for each other."

"Are you aware of any instances where your husband had an interaction with Brigid's ex-husband, the victim, Lawrence Tanner?"

She shook her head. "No, I wasn't familiar with Mr. Tanner. We knew Brigid had been divorced but not anything more than that. It came as a horrible surprise to all of us when Jason was arrested. An even bigger surprise when it turned out that the victim was Brigid's ex-husband," Clara said.

"Do you think your husband is capable of committing a crime of this nature, taking the life of another human being?" Jemimah asked.

Clara's voice cracked. "My husband is a kind and caring person, who would never harm another human being, let alone in this manner. He is generous, compassionate and honorable, contrary to what the news media has made him out to be," she said. "Because of all the publicity that surrounds the case, he has already been tried and convicted."

Jemimah scooted her seat back and stood. She let out a long breath of air. "Clara, thank you for your honesty. I have a few more questions to ask Brigid and then we should be finished here," she said.

Clara reached over to hug her. This time Jemimah didn't resist. Katie felt a tear form in her eye.

a period of courting takes place, and then a ceremony joins them in matrimony. We couldn't have a real wedding because only the first wife is the legal one," she said. "I wasn't looking forward to meeting the other wives, and less of becoming part of the group."

"And did that matrimonial ceremony take place?"

Brigid let out a barely audible sigh. "No, as I said, we had made a plan to eventually leave the other wives and start a life together, so we would then be married. We saw no point in being part of a ceremony which would mean nothing in the long run," she said.

"When your ex-husband, Lawrence Tanner, found out about your plans to marry into a polygamist sect, what happened?"

"He threw a bloody fit. For a time after the divorce became final, he kept trying to convince me that I should come back to him, and that things would be different. He was incensed that I would already be with someone else so soon after we broke up," she said.

"Did you know your ex-husband was going to be in the Santa Fe area? Had he contacted you for any reason?" Jemimah said.

"No, I don't think he knew where we had moved to. We hadn't been in contact for some time. I knew nothing about it until the officers came to our home and Jason was arrested."

"Do you think Jason Hodge was aware that your ex-husband was in town?"

"I can't see where he would be. He never answered the phone or made any calls except to obtain lumber and other building materials, Most of our construction supplies were arranged for by phone and for a long time now, he spent his days remodeling the compound to make it more livable for the four of us. He rarely went into town except to take us shopping on Fridays," she said. "He was very budget-minded and made sure we only bought the necessary staples."

Jemimah continued to ask questions along the same line.

Chapter Thirty

WHEN CLARA HODGE left the room, Katie took a break to give Jemimah a moment to herself. She returned with the next wife.

Brigid Hodge walked into the room, her head high, exuding an air of confidence not present in her sister wives. Jemimah believed this wife to be more worldly, more aware of things around her. It was obvious that, unlike the other women, she had not grown up in a sheltered environment.

"Have a seat, Brigid. I just have a few more questions, and they involve your relationship with both the victim and the suspect."

She sat at the edge of the chair and looked straight at Jemimah. Katie resumed recording.

"How long after you met Jason Hodge did you decide to pursue a relationship?"

"I believe I mentioned earlier that we started seeing each other before anyone knew about it. We were keeping it secret while my divorce was finalized," she said.

"Why so secretive?" Jemimah said.

"According to the way things had been done in the past, I'm talking about new wives being introduced into the group,

"Had you recently changed your mind about being a fourth wife?"

"Not completely. Quite frankly, I was just frustrated about Jason having to spend time with these other women, who more than usual seemed to be volleying for his attention, but he kept assuring me that things were going to work out between us," she said. "It was necessary for me to participate in family dinners with all of them and being limited to see him only one night a week. That became a bone of contention with us."

"Do you think Jason might have believed that if he didn't follow up on his promises, you would return to your ex-husband and that he killed him to keep that from happening?"

Brigid's hands went to her mouth. "How can you say that?"

"I'm not saying that," Jemimah said. "He is the main suspect. Perhaps that might be motive enough for the police, especially if they think Jason changed his mind and believed you were leaving him to return to your ex-husband, the victim in this case."

Brigid spread her arms, gripped the desk and leaned forward. "Look, Lawrence was angry, I'll admit that. Even after he became engaged to his girlfriend, he was still trying to get me to change my mind. He said I needed to come to my senses. I told him I had made up my mind, and I wasn't going to change it," Brigid said. "After that I changed cell phones and don't know whether or not he continued to try."

"Do you know why he was so insistent, being that the divorce was in process and you were with another man?" Jemimah asked.

"Because a divorce was going to affect his status in the church and he would rather pretend to be happy than to actually be happy. I couldn't do that," she said. "Our marriage had been a charade, with me having to act as though I fit into the role of a Mormon wife. I was over it."

"On another subject, did you ever wonder if his fiancée, Eliza Simpson, might have been aware of his interaction with you?" Jemimah said.

"Why do you ask?"

"Just covering all bases. You mentioned you knew her."

"I knew of her, but didn't know her personally. Small town, lots of gossip. I'm sure she's a very nice person and I assume probably more suited to being a Mormon wife than I was."

"I have to ask this next question. Did you have anything to do with Lawrence Tanner's murder, whether by committing the act yourself or having knowledge of who killed him?" Jemimah said.

Her eyes grew wide. "I certainly did not. In the first place, I am not a violent person, and secondly I'm offended by that question."

"I understand, but it's part of my job to ask difficult questions." Jemimah nodded toward Katie, who turned the recorder to off. "I think we're done here, Brigid. If I think of anything else, I might give you a call, if that's all right."

"Yes, certainly. And I hope you don't mind my saying, but you do resemble Clara in many ways. I'm glad you got to see each other, even if under these circumstances," she said.

Jemimah shook her hand. "Thank you again for coming."

When the women had left her office, Jemimah plopped into her chair. Katie patted her on the hand. "You doing all right?"

"Other than feeling like I've just been mowed over by a tractor, yes," Jemimah said. "Let's get out of here. I need some air."

On the drive home, she speed-dialed her therapist, Jerry Cade, to schedule an appointment. The events of the past two weeks had left her in a state of angst, and she knew it would soon boil over into her personal life.

Chapter Thirty-One

T HAT FRIDAY AFTERNOON, Eliza Simpson was browsing through the nightlife section of the *Pasatiempo*, the newspaper's weekly culture section. There were a number of gallery openings, and she hadn't yet had an opportunity to wander up Canyon Road and check out the many offerings. She checked at the front desk and learned the well-publicized art district of Santa Fe was about six blocks away. She decided the exercise would be a good way to work off some of the indulgences she engaged in on her several visits to the French pastry shop a block away from the hotel.

The friendly atmosphere of the galleries she visited left Eliza exhilarated. She never imagined a city of this size would provide such a doorway to experience so much incredible art. Having walked back to the mouth of Canyon Road, she stopped to rest on a concrete bench. She looked down at her throbbing feet and decided to call Uber and catch a short ride back to her room. On the way to her hotel, she asked the driver to leave her at the La Fonda Hotel so she could have an early dinner before the place filled up.

She waited only a few minutes before she was seated at a small table in La Plazuela, the main dining room of the hotel.

While she waited for her meal, she snapped a few quick photos of the painted glass door and window panels which encircled the room. After dinner, she glanced at her watch. It was almost eight o'clock. She rounded the corner and walked through the lobby. The hotel lounge was on the east corner.

Eliza was drawn to the sound of the music and the laughter and camaraderie of the crowd.

"Why not?" she told herself. It reminded her of the previous years, before she decided to convert to Mormonism to marry Lawrence Tanner. She hadn't danced or had a drink of alcohol since then. She spotted a small table in the corner. The barmaid quickly wiped the table, motioned her to sit and placed a paper napkin in front of her.

Eliza placed her purse on the floor next to her chair and ordered a glass of white wine. A grin of delight covered her face as she took her first sip.

The band performed a series of currently popular songs along with a medley of country western music, which the crowd seemed to prefer. Eliza found herself clapping with the crowd when the lead singer hit a long high note on one of Blake Shelton's songs.

She took another sip of her drink and looked around the room. It had been a long time since she'd been in any type of social situation that involved liquor, dancing and music. *Who am I kidding,* she thought. *I was so intent on participating in everything necessary to convert my religion to please Lawrence, I lost track of who I really am.*

She looked up to see a tall, blue-eyed, sandy-haired gentleman standing next to her table.

"It's a bit crowded in here. Would you mind terribly if I shared your table?" he said.

Caught off guard, Eliza wasn't sure how to respond.

"I'm sorry," he said. "I've embarrassed you. I can see you're not used to strange men coming on to you."

"No, no," she said. "My mind was a million miles away. Of course you can sit here."

Chapter Thirty-Two

HE SMILED A toothy smile at her. "At least let me buy you a drink," he said.

While the handsome stranger made his way to place their order at the bar, Eliza reached into her purse for her compact. With her index finger she wiped stray mascara from under her eyes and touched up her lipstick. She took one last look, snapped the compact shut and returned it to her purse.

Drinks in hand, he set one in front of her, then pulled the chair out and sat down. Dave McPherson leaned across and slid a business card toward her. "Just so you don't think I'm some kind of serial killer," he said.

Eliza laughed. "You have such a sincere look on your face, how can I not believe you. Another thing, I would imagine this hotel is kind of expensive for a killer to hang out in."

He grinned. "Not that a pretty lady like you would know anything about serial killers, but I have to say that my expense account barely covers meals, let alone a three hundred dollar a night room."

When the tempo of the music slowed down, he asked her to dance. He twirled her around the floor for several sets and then escorted her back to the table.

"This might seem a bit forward," he said. "But would you like to get out of here? It's still early enough to enjoy seeing the plaza by moonlight."

She hesitated for only an instant and then nodded. They made their way down the hallway through the lobby. He reached ahead and opened the big brass doors at the exit. "After you, Madame," he said.

Eliza threw a sideways glance in his direction, flattered to be receiving such attention from a total stranger. It was out of character for her to allow herself to be placed in such a position. After all, she had spent the previous year been schooled in the mores of the Mormon Church, which were to lead to her conversion. *What the heck,* she thought. *That train has left the station.* It was then she could see no point in continuing on when she returned home.

Dave gently took her arm as they crossed San Francisco Street. They walked along the covered portals circling the square, stopping at each window to look at the myriad offerings.

"I can see why tourists are drawn here," she said. "It's quite mesmerizing." She pointed at a chunky turquoise and silver necklace in the window of the corner shop. "I'm sure that would add ten pounds around my neck."

"I think you're more a ruby and diamond kind of girl," he chuckled. "At least that's what I think you would look best in."

Lost in conversation, they circled around the block, passing in front of the church. Walking in front of Rainbow Man Gallery, they stopped to look at the colorful figures in the window. When they turned onto Lincoln Avenue, Eliza pointed to the Anasazi Hotel. "This is where I'm staying for a few days," she said.

"Are you up for a nightcap, I hope?" he said.

She glanced down at her watch. "It's really late," she said, looking up at him. He was at least a foot taller than she was. She liked the way he craned his neck to look at her, as if gazing down at something special.

"You're smiling," he said. "What are you thinking?"

Eliza felt her cheeks redden. "Oh, just one of those silly things women think about when they encounter a handsome stranger in their midst."

He squeezed her hand. "And what is that? That we'll probably never see each other again?"

"Something like that," she said.

"Well, then. I suggest we make the most of it. Can I talk you into lunch tomorrow, or maybe dinner?" He paused. "Or both?"

"Let me think about it," she said.

He thanked her for a delightful evening, as he put it, and leaned down to kiss her on the forehead.

"Eliza, I hope you will consider spending time with me again. I enjoyed your company and would like to see more of you. I need to take an afternoon drive sometime soon to Truchas, a village on the way to Taos, and I could sure use the company for that and checking out the local restaurants," he said, "if you're up for it."

She hesitated, and he smiled at her. "You can sleep on it and text me in the morning. My number's on the card I gave you."

He walked her into the lobby and then turned to walk away.

She gazed after him as the elevator doors closed. Although she would have liked to spend more time with this man, she knew it wouldn't look right for her to be dating someone so soon. But she tucked his card in her wallet, just in case.

Chapter Thirty-Three

DETECTIVE ROMERO SPENT the entire weekend investigating a drug bust the sheriff corralled him into. Jemimah was aware how much the personnel shortage and lack of honeymoon had affected their daily life. The homicide case involving her father had also done a number on her emotions.

It was the beginning of a new week, a glorious Monday morning. Jemimah smiled as she parked her car next to the curb in front of Ecco, a trendy coffee house on East Marcy Street. She walked past the gelato counter and the pastry section, and ordered a half-caff Americano. While she waited, she chatted with the handsome barista. With a stir and a flourish, he handed her the to-go cup and smiled. "On the house," he said. She thanked him and pushed a few bills into the tip jar. She loaded the container with cream, secured the lid and reached for her keys as she headed out the door. She took a sip of the creamy liquid and sighed.

"Mmmm. What a great way to start the day."

Once in her vehicle Jemimah reached for her cell and texted Katie to let her know she had an appointment and would be late coming in. She buckled up and eased out of the parking space while the car behind waited patiently to take over. She drove east across town, south past Museum Hill and onto Old Santa Fe Trail. For the next five miles, the roadside was filled with newly-bloomed wildflowers, the result of early spring rains in the area. She would have liked to pull over and enjoy the moment, but a quick glance at her phone reminded her she was already running late.

Today would be the first time her appointment would be at her therapist's eastside home. Dr. Jerry Cade retired from practice the previous year, but still saw some of his patients on an emergency basis. Jemimah considered this time in her life to resemble an emergency. On the road up ahead she saw the bright blue mailbox, turned left onto a narrow dirt road and traveled up a steep hill. Had she not known there would be a house at the end of the road, it would have come as a big surprise.

The circular drive in front of the two-story adobe house was paved with red brick and bordered by a two foot wall, along which colorful blooms sprouted from the gardens. Large terracotta bowls flanked the front porch, adding additional bursts of color. Jemimah parked her car, and took a quick look in the mirror. She sipped the last of the coffee, reached across the seat for a bottle of water and walked up the drive.

She rang the doorbell and was greeted by an older Mexican woman, who she assumed was the housekeeper. She directed Jemimah to a large room with high ceilings and wood beams. The walls were an off-white diamond finish and the massive fireplace sported a contrasting red oxide color. The room was decorated with contemporary Native American paintings and carved Kachina figures. Comfortable couches and Navajo rugs completed the décor.

She walked across the room and sat in a leather chair. The housekeeper informed her Dr. Cade would be in shortly and offered her a beverage, but Jemimah thanked her and pointed to the bottle of water. She leaned back and rested her feet on the hassock while she waited. So many things were running through her mind, from the lack of a proper honeymoon to the meetings with the women from her past. She closed her eyes to put things in the order she wanted to discuss them.

"Jemimah?"

She jumped with a start when she heard his voice. "Oh, Dr. Cade, I must have drifted off for a moment," she said, her cheeks flushed.

He laughed and leaned down to buss her cheek. "The air up this high seems to do that a lot."

She started to get up. Dr. Cade raised the palm of his hand in her direction. "No, Jemimah. Let's stay here. My office is much too stuffy. I prefer the light and the view from this room."

She relaxed back in the chair. He thanked the housekeeper for the coffee she set in front of him and asked that he not be disturbed.

He turned to Jemimah, who, with little prompting, talked non-stop for thirty minutes about everything that came to mind. She paused and took a breath. "Wow, Jerry, I didn't realize I was holding that much in."

"Sounds like you've had a lot to deal with. How are you feeling at this moment?" he said.

"As though I've been bombarded with remembrances that I would have preferred stayed where they were. I'm not sure if I should be happy or sad."

"Why is that?"

"I've gone all these years not having to deal with circumstances that led up to my running away from a home situation which I perceived was going to bring me nothing but painful heartache. All these years, I have been my own mother and father, having endured hardships, hunger, stress, a failed marriage to a fellow student at UCLA. I did everything for myself that I believed my parents should have done. I fed and clothed myself and paid my own way through college and grad school."

Dr. Cade stopped her in mid-sentence. "How did you feel when you saw these women for the first time, Jemimah?"

She shook her head. "I was a wreck. Those years were

traumatizing enough and after working through it for so long I believed the past no longer had a hold on me. And then, there I was, facing the woman who did not stand up to my father when he decided to leave the Mormon Church and join the FLDS."

"Do you really believe she could have changed his mind? Are you still angry at her?" he said.

"I was, but after listening to the four wives talk about how well he's treated them and how they've never lacked for anything, I realized that was her life, not mine." She looked across at him. "Don't get me wrong, I feel sorry that she was deprived of the life she initially signed up for, but I also believe that it was her choice to stay in that situation."

"Let me ask you this. How do you remember your parents getting along when it was just you and then your brother?"

Jemimah inclined her head. "They seemed happy. She was a good wife and mother, and he was a good provider."

"And after they left the Mormon Church and joined the FLDS; what was her reaction then?"

"I don't think she was pleased about that," Jemimah said. "She appeared crushed when he introduced the prospect of adding a wife. My mother smiled through it, but then when my father started entertaining the idea of a third wife a short time later, I think she resigned herself to the fact that things would never be the same."

"This is how you truly feel, that she could have changed the situation if she had spoken up?" he said.

"I was twelve when this happened. I still believed that a strong faith could move mountains. That's what we had been taught in church."

"And you believed you could change the way your father was thinking? You were twelve. Do you still believe that?"

She sighed. "I'm not sure what I believe anymore."

Dr. Cade leaned forward and looked her straight in the face. "You need to stop denying your feelings, Jemimah. Even with all your degrees, everything you've learned about the psyche, you're still human. Nobody is going to fault you for admitting you're angry for the way things turned out. For Chrissake, you were a child. You had no control over what the adults in the family did, the decisions they made. In the long run, due to your tenacity, your life probably turned out better than it would have had you remained in the group your father gravitated to," he said.

Jemimah felt her neck muscles tighten. "Yes, I'm sure that's true, but part of me is so incensed about his self-serving and narcissistic demeanor that sometimes I can't think straight. If all of this would have never happened, I would have had the benefit of growing up with my mother as the only wife, and my father at her side."

He shrugged his shoulders. "But that didn't happen. Now, have you seen your father yet?"

"No, and I'm not sure if there will be a need to do that. In a way I was relieved he hired an attorney, so the DA would have to petition the Court to allow him to undergo any of the type of profiling that my job calls for."

"What would you say to him if he was seated across from you right now?"

"Oh, probably nothing at all. I do believe that I have always resigned myself to the fact that nothing I said, then or now, would serve to have changed anything that happened," she said.

He laughed and spun his chair to face her. "Did you hear what you just said? Your defense mechanism just bullied its way to the forefront and modified your thought pattern. What would you really say, Jemimah?"

She paused for a long moment. "That I'm so damned angry that I can hardly contain myself. That his selfishness and self-centered conduct caused my mother enormous grief to lose him as a husband and me to lose both of them as parents. By the time I was eight, I had read the entire Book of Mormon, stories of ancient Israelite peoples led by God to the Americas. Our family was entrenched in the religion, devoting their spare moments to worship and learning. I was taken away from the ritual of the church, from all my friends and schoolmates, and everything in our lives was replaced by the confusion of the Fundamentalist sect we were thrown into."

"So now, what do you think the real reason was for your wanting to leave the situation?"

"Because my father determined that as soon as my skin condition was cleared up, I would be more marriageable to someone of his choice. That as his daughter, or maybe as a woman, I was expendable. It didn't matter what I wanted. The men in this group lived a double standard entrenched in their beliefs. They were privileged. Women were not. My mother was caught up in the rules and demands and my father made all the decisions, so she would not have been able to walk away."

Jemimah paused. "My God, for a moment I felt as though I was listening to someone else's drama."

"Let me ask you this, Jemimah. What are you afraid of? That you might realize how much you missed a normal family life and how angry you are that it didn't happen that way? It is okay to be angry. It is okay to admit that you are human, and as humans, that's what we do. We think, we feel, we express our emotions, we act on impulse. We make mistakes. None of these things are wrong."

Jemimah was quiet. Dr. Cade gave her a moment to soak it all in before he continued.

"I admire you so much for having been able to not only survive being on your own at such a young age, but having the tenacity and strength of spirit to make something of yourself. As a licensed psychologist myself, it is mind-boggling to me how you navigated through it all, graduated from college and earned a PhD. Do you know what kind of inner resolve and determination that must have taken?" He shook his head in awe.

Jemimah smiled weakly. "I guess that's why I went into my field, partially to understand what had happened in my own life, but also to assure myself I had not made a mistake in running away. Maybe now I can relegate all those troublesome memories into the compartments of my brain where they can be shredded."

Dr. Cade chuckled. "That's an excellent idea. A very wise teacher once said to me that in order to go forward, you have to go backwards. What is it people these days say? Been there, done that. And you certainly have." He glanced at his watch. "As much as I'd like to spend another hour with you, Jemimah, I have a patient scheduled."

Her chest heaved. "It's always too short a time, but I too have to get back to work."

As Dr. Cade walked her out to her car, she turned to embrace him. "Thank you, Jerry. I am grateful for having spent this time with you."

He smiled. "As am I, and I hope you and that detective husband of yours are able to take off on that honeymoon very soon. Walking along the beach in Mexico is a great place to put things in perspective."

Chapter Thirty-Four

———•———

THAT AFTERNOON, DETECTIVE Romero left a message on Jemimah's cell. "Hi, Sweet Thing. Sorry I missed you. I just picked McCabe up at the airport in Santa Fe. He's just back from a three day trip to New York, and I'm going to drop him off at the house in town. See you after work."

McCabe lifted his suitcase into the back seat of Romero's cruiser. He pulled himself into the passenger seat and buckled himself in.

"Rick, thanks so much for doing this. You can drop me off at the dealership to pick up my vehicle. That will save us a trip. Couldn't get ahold of Laura, she wasn't picking up. Probably out in the garden checking the azaleas. She's a nut for flowers. I love that about her," McCabe said.

On the twelve mile drive from the airport, McCabe talked about his appearance on the *Today Show*, which had become a monthly venue to discuss the progress of the treasure hunt and for him to give another clue to listeners and potential treasure hunters. Before he left, he was bombarded by reporters seeking additional clues on the elusive treasure. "I just smiled and said I had no further comment."

"Sounds like you had a productive trip, and based on the

extra luggage you slipped into the back, you came with more than you left," Romero laughed.

"Yeah, I make it a point to stop by Laura's favorite stores and pick up everything on her list. She likes to stay fashionable and New York is the place to accomplish that. Don't know how many more trips I'll need to take. Someone better find that treasure before I'm too old to enjoy it."

"From what you say, you've provided a number of additional clues since the hunt started," Romero mused.

"Yes, and if someone would just go through all the clues, including the ones in the book, put them in the right order, they'd have a pretty clear roadmap that would lead them right to the location," McCabe said.

"Good thing you don't talk in your sleep, *Hombre*. Someone could bug your bedroom and maybe get a few more clues," he chuckled.

"Laura says I'm a snorer, not a talker," McCabe laughed.

The traffic from the airport made the going a bit slow. Romero brought him up to date on the homicide. No news wasn't necessarily good news. The more time that elapsed, the more chance the killer would get away with it.

He dropped McCabe off at the Lexus dealership on Cerrillos Road, turned around and headed back out the highway. McCabe had to wait another twenty minutes before his vehicle was delivered. He looked at his watch. Traffic permitting, he would be home just in time to unpack, spin through a quick shower and make their dinner reservations.

***

Laura McCabe's feet were propped on the leather ottoman as she relaxed back on the recliner in the living room of the couple's Canyon Road residence. She had spent the afternoon in the garden and decided to take a short nap before getting ready for dinner. Tim was taking her to Café Martín, one of her favorite restaurants. It appeared to her that from time to time he had a tendency to become so deeply involved with the Sheriff's department he spent little time at home. She was looking forward to a quiet evening with her husband and was waiting for him to call so she could pick him up at the airport.

She leaned her head back and closed her eyes. Rosa, the housekeeper, had almost completed her weekly chores and would see herself out. Earlier in the day the rug service had returned the Navajo rugs to the living room floor and hung the red and black Chief's Blanket back on the wall. She smiled as her breath slowed and she dropped off to sleep.

Laura was deeply relaxed when a loud thud pulled her out of her slumber. Momentarily disoriented, she gazed around the room and saw someone standing outside the patio doors which had been left slightly ajar when she came in from the garden.

She sat up abruptly and reached for her phone. She tried to dial but noticed the phone had been off. No wonder she hadn't heard from Tim. The intruder was across the room in seconds; slapping the phone from her hands. She screamed and turned to run toward the hall. He overtook her, pulled her back into the living room and pushed her to the couch and ordered her to sit down.

She couldn't stop shaking. "Who are you? What do you want?" She stammered. She thought she had seen him recently, as the man who wouldn't take no for an answer when he wanted to interact with her husband about the treasure hunt in which he was involved. She didn't have a chance.

"Shut up and don't bother screaming. Nobody can hear you," he said, releasing his grip on her wrist.

She started to protest and felt something being pushed over her face. She felt a wave of dizziness and then everything went black.

Moments earlier as the housekeeper was leaving through the alarmed gates, she stopped midway to allow the heavy afternoon traffic to pass. A tall man wearing a dark shirt and a baseball cap stood by the mailbox as if waiting to cross in front of her car. As she looked to check traffic again before moving completely out of the driveway onto Canyon Road, she saw the man sprint along the side of her car and through the gates just as they closed. With her car already in motion as she moved into traffic, she kept her eyes on the rearview mirror and saw him run toward the house. In a panic, she pulled into a driveway about a block away and reached for her phone.

McCabe was maneuvering through the heavy traffic when he saw Rosa's name come up on his cell phone. He tapped the speaker button. "Rosa, did you need something? I was just on my way home."

"Mr. Tim...a very bad man is at the house...I saw him run through the gates," she said.

He jerked the wheel to the right and pulled to a stop on the side of the road. "Slow down, Rosa. Tell me what happened," he said.

Rosa explained what she had seen. "There was so much traffic I couldn't turn my car around and go back to the house. Mrs. McCabe was taking a nap in the living room when I left. I didn't know what to do. I was afraid he would hurt her if I called 911." She started to cry.

"You did the right thing, Rosa. I'm on my way. Don't try to go back to the house," he said, and hung up the phone. His tires screeched as he pulled back onto the road and sped out.

Detective Romero was about to stop by his office after dropping McCabe off when the County 911 dispatcher called.

"Hey, what's up?" he said.

"Detective Romero, we just received an emergency alarm notification from the McCabe residence. The call came from one of those gadgets where you press the button if you're in some sort of trouble. However, it appeared more to be a test run, as the beep only lasted for a few seconds," she said.

"Yeah, McCabe mentioned they were thinking about signing on with a local company, but they hadn't worked out the specifics yet. I just dropped him off and he should be close to home by now. Let me take care of it from this end and I'll get back to you," he said.

He hung up and tried McCabe's number, waited until the

call went to message and then tried again. It wasn't like Tim not to pick up. He turned the cruiser around and headed back down Highway 14 to the residence, sirens whirling. He called Santa Fe City Police and asked them to meet him near there, but not run their sirens as he wasn't sure exactly what was going on. For all he knew it was a false alarm but he couldn't take a chance of his best friend getting hurt.

Chapter Thirty-Five

T HE PROPERTY GATES slid open and McCabe sped through the driveway. He jumped from the driver's seat and ran to the front door. The security lock had been activated. It could only be opened from inside. He banged on the door and shouted Laura's name. No answer.

He spotted the open patio door and let himself in. He crossed the living room into the hallway calling her name. Nothing again. He felt his insides twist. He was in a panic. He blew out a breath of air. *Where was she?*

Minutes passed as he went from room to room. A wave of terror gripped him as he turned the knob on the door into the studio. He slowly pushed the door open. The next sound he heard was the recognizable click of the hammer of a pistol. As he turned his head he recognized the man who had come to their door a few weeks before and refused to leave. He was also the subject of McCabe's recent request for a restraining order, Wendell Sherman.

Sherman was a man in his early fifties with dark brooding eyes and a military style haircut. He was wearing dirty sneakers and faded jeans. A snug-fitting t-shirt accentuated his muscular physique. He was holding a Colt 1911 in his hand.

"Put your hands behind you," he said.

McCabe complied and stood still as his hands were bound. His gaze shifted across the room. Laura was strapped to a chair, a gag over her mouth.

He pushed McCabe against the wall. "I can see the gears clicking in your head, McCabe," Sherman said. "Don't try anything you'll be sorry for. I'm a trained marksman and you'd be dead on the floor before you could count to three."

McCabe glanced over at Laura, her blue eyes large with fright. "Let my wife go. She has nothing to do with this."

Sherman laughed and walked over to Laura and playfully tousled her hair. "She's my security blanket. An assurance that you're going to tell me what I need to know," Sherman said.

McCabe stared him in the eyes. "What are you after, jewelry, cash, what?"

"You know damned well what I'm after. That treasure chest of yours. I know it's not buried anywhere. That's a story you people concocted for the publicity. You've got it stashed somewhere so you can look at it every day," Sherman said.

Having had several confrontations with this individual in the past, McCabe decided it might be best to go along with his story, since he'd learned from experience there wasn't much he could say to convince him otherwise. He pulled his shoulders back.

"What's it going to take to persuade you the box is nowhere around here? Maybe you hit the nail on the head. It was all a story, and we've had a good run," McCabe said. "Lot of suckers around looking for the gold at the end of the rainbow."

Sherman pushed the pistol against the tip of McCabe's nose. "Don't try to con me, McCabe. I saw the photos in your book and on your blog. I have no doubt the chest exists, and that you were bullshitting about having buried it. Nobody is that big of a fool," Sherman said.

McCabe tried to placate him. "You're wrong, Sherman. Even after the publicity stunt had run its course, the story kept building up momentum. I have nothing to show you," he said.

"Maybe this will convince you otherwise." He moved toward Laura and reached for her hand. She smothered a cry as he twisted her wrist.

McCabe lurched forward. "Leave her alone!" he said. "All right, all right...leave my wife here and I'll take you to it. The chest is about twenty miles from here, hidden in a cave."

Sherman cackled. "You think I'm that stupid? She'll call the cops the minute we're gone. She goes where we go." He released her from the chair, bound her hands in front and shuffled the couple toward the door. "In case there's anyone around, we're going to walk out quietly, get in your car, and drive out of here like everything is fine." He grabbed a scarf from the hallway and draped it over Laura's hands.

Out on the driveway the trio paused for a moment as Sherman pulled open the side door of the Hummer and motioned for Laura to get in.

"If you expect me to drive, you need to free my hands," McCabe said. "The keys are in my right hand pocket if you're planning on driving. Then again, it might be better if you drove."

Sherman pushed Laura onto the seat and closed the door. "I'll be riding shotgun, McCabe. One eye on you and the other on your wife. Make a false move and she won't live to see tomorrow." He untied McCabe and stood close to the open door of the Hummer.

McCabe inhaled deeply and slid into the driver's seat. He cranked up the engine and drove along the circular driveway to the street where he scanned the area as the iron gate slid open. He thought for sure the test signal from his personal alarm had been picked up by now. As he drove out onto Canyon Road, he thought he recognized two of Romero's unmarked Chevys parked at the rose park near the corner of Garcia Street.

As McCabe motored down the road toward the highway, his mind was racing. His grip on the steering wheel was tight enough to turn his knuckles white. He was biding for time by pretending the treasure was hidden out on the Indian ruins at

San Lazaro. He didn't have much longer to formulate a plan. He just knew he had to get Sherman as far away from Laura as possible. He sure as hell wasn't going to let anything happen to her. He was more concerned for Laura's safety than his own.

The trip would provide about forty-five minutes tops to figure out how to persuade this joker he was taking him to the right place. The guy looked like a nut-case and it might not take much to set him off.

McCabe checked on Laura through the rear view mirror. He could see the terror in her eyes.

Chapter Thirty-Six

THIRTY MINUTES BEFORE, a few blocks from the McCabe residence, Romero had assembled a SWAT team. Having been in the McCabe home many times over the years, he was fairly certain he could draw an accurate map of the oversized lot. He positioned two officers on the roof of the house next door. Detective Martinez had just returned to duty and spent a few minutes recording images with a telephoto lens.

Romero's radio crackled. "Boss, there's some activity in front of the house. Guy with a gun leading McCabe and his wife to the Hummer. Just sent a video to your phone," Martinez said.

Romero pulled up the images and studied the photos. "This confirms the guy is the one McCabe was seeking the TRO on. Let them go out the gate. We can't take the chance of either of them being killed if we show up," Romero said. "I'll take one of the unmarked and follow McCabe. We might have to pick this guy off at some point. Take a couple of guys with you from the SWAT team in the other unmarked."

Romero waited until the Hummer had traveled a few blocks and he pulled off from St. Francis Drive onto the road and followed for about ten miles. When the Hummer pulled onto the Highway 14 exit, Romero realized they were headed to Cerrillos. He debated whether they were going to the ranch or the Indian Ruins. He radioed Detective Martinez and gave him the details.

"I'm going to follow behind for a bit more. You go a ways past the turnoff and wait until I can determine exactly where they're headed."

McCabe flipped the turn signals when he reached County Road 65A. The road turned to gravel for the next two miles and wound its way under the railroad trestle.

Wendell Sherman shifted in the passenger seat. "You know where the hell you going? Don't look like there's much out here," he grunted.

McCabe glanced in his direction. "Keep your shirt on. This turns into a private road once we cross the Galisteo River coming up. Then it's still another five miles or so in. You're not going to see much around here but coyotes," he said. As they crossed under the railroad trestle, he could see there were no fresh tracks on the road. He had hoped somehow Romero might have gone on ahead but then realized Sherman would have noticed the tire marks and maybe even the dust if there was anyone a short distance out in front.

Sherman interrupted his thoughts. "How much longer? We're already out in the damned boonies."

McCabe gestured with his hand. "Just up ahead. We still have one more cattle guard to cross before we get to the main gate. It's all private property, you know."

He drove slowly on the pitted washboard road and five minutes later pressed a button on the dash to open the gate. He pulled ahead as the gate closed behind him and stopped the vehicle alongside a grove of trees and cut the engine.

He turned to face Sherman. "We'll have to walk a short ways around that hill. Can't drive up to it," McCabe said.

Sherman unclipped his seat belt. "About time," he said. "You got a shovel?"

"Don't need one," said McCabe.

Pistol in hand, Sherman climbed out of the vehicle and walked around to the driver's side and motioned for McCabe to get out.

"Don't try anything funny, McCabe. My pistol has a hair trigger. Wouldn't want it to go off by accident."

McCabe slid down slowly until his boots touched the hard earth. Sherman pushed him ahead and opened the passenger side. He reached for Laura's elbow, intending to pull her out.

"Leave her here," McCabe said. She'll just slow us down. She might stumble and fall. Besides, with her hands tied she can't do anything from the back seat. She's not going to get loose and run off and call the cops."

Sherman snorted. "All right, but hurry up. This has already taken too long."

McCabe pointed to a spot up ahead. "Just a little over that rise there," he said.

Laura sat in silence as she watched her husband and their abductor walk out of sight. The windows on the Hummer were barely open. She tugged at the rope on her wrists. Her hands burned and ached, but she persisted. Remembering her scoutmaster days, she knew a little about knots and checked to see what style Sherman had used. She prayed she could loosen the rope enough to get free. She took a deep breath and thanked God the chloroform had finally worn off.

Laura's faith had always been strong. She knew this situation would require every ounce of strength she could muster. "Come on, Laura," she encouraged herself as her heart pounded into overdrive.

Chapter Thirty-Seven

Having followed behind until McCabe's Hummer took the turn off the highway, Romero radioed Detective Martinez to continue down Highway 14 and bypass the county road leading to McCabe's property. Martinez acknowledged and pulled over to the side of the road and unfolded a map of the area. Detective Chacon joined him.

"Bad news, Artie. The boss said for us to stand back. From where he thinks McCabe has taken the guy, they would be able to see any vehicles approach," Martinez said. "That might cause a hell of a lot of trouble for McCabe if we're spotted."

With his finger, Detective Chacon traced a circle on the map. "So if McCabe led the guy here to the northeast corner of the ruins, how close can we get? Isn't there a back road? Remember last year when Romero's ex had his brother Carlos trapped in the old convent ruins somewhere around there?"

Martinez traced a line on the map. "Yeah, you're right, Artie. We went down Highway 14 another six miles or so and turned here on the dead end, which even though it's marked that way, it goes on for some time." He folded up the map, put the unmarked vehicle in drive and pulled onto the highway.

"I'll radio Romero and let him know where we're headed

and assure him that Officer Davis here can pick a fly off a rock at 1500 yards," Chacon said.

"Seriously?" said Martinez.

"Damned right. Iraqi war veteran. Been with our SWAT team for about a year now. Invaluable."

"Okay, guys, you know I'm sitting in the back seat," said Officer Davis. "Enough on the flattery. Let's get this guy captured or dead."

Martinez headed south, traveling at breakneck speed. They drove five miles past the Town of Cerrillos and turned on State Road 55C. They followed the dead-end dirt road for a mile and then pulled in close to an embankment. By the time they unloaded their gear, Romero radioed to say he was on his way.

They trekked across about an acre of rough terrain, skirting arroyos and ledges. The heavy gravel crunched beneath their feet as they approached the ancient convent building up ahead. A stream trickled slowly through Del Chorro Creek and ran alongside the path as they walked parallel to the edge of the high canyon walls. Half a mile later, everything flattened out into smaller rolling hills. Based on prior experience, the detectives knew they would be easily spotted if they moved any closer than the old church ruins.

***

Laura McCabe's forehead was dripping with sweat. The hot sun had been bearing down on the Hummer for more than fifteen minutes. She stared out through the top of the barely cracked window. She could see McCabe and their captor standing by the base of the monolithic outcropping known as Medicine Rock. Her husband was pointing to some object out of her vision.

Her wrists were raw and blistered. With sore fingers she continued to work the knots on the rope. She could feel them starting to loosen. As she pulled faster, her fingers started to bleed. Time was running out. She knew the treasure was more than five hundred miles from Santa Fe and knowing her husband, he was trying to save her from harm by bringing Sherman out here. She prayed Detective Romero had picked up on the plan. That might be their only hope.

Another pull on the rope and it gave way. She glanced out the window again to make sure they were still out of sight. She pulled herself over to the front seat. She knew McCabe kept a pistol underneath the driver's side. Her hand moved quickly under the seat. She sighed with relief. *Thank God!* She removed the gun from the holster and clicked the magazine in. She quietly opened the passenger side door and slid out, all the time terrified of being discovered. She ran up the incline and alongside the back of Medicine Rock into the cover of a stand of salt cedars. Her shoulders tensed as she moved nearer to the edge, which would put her directly behind the mouth of the cave.

Working her way through the dense foliage, thorny bushes scratched deeply into her arms. Juniper and chamisa were in full bloom and as the breeze floated the pollen visibly around her, Laura worked to stifle a sneeze. Stepping carefully to not make a sound, she continued to move forward, inches at a time. And then she heard the loud and angry voices. She drew a deep breath to steady her shaky nerves.

Chapter Thirty-Eight

MINUTES BEFORE, ROMERO pulled his vehicle in behind Martinez's car and parked. He killed the engine, reached for his service pistol, and got out of the car, carefully closing the door. He radioed Martinez to determine their location and then headed up the rocky path, hurrying to catch up. It was a grueling span of fifteen minutes. The three men were gathered on the side of the old convent building, both Martinez and Chacon were on the ground peering through binoculars. Detective Martinez turned to see Romero and motioned him ahead.

He handed Romero a set of binoculars. "Hey, Boss, take a look. McCabe and the guy are standing in front of the cave. Guy looks pretty angry," he said.

Romero lowered himself to the ground and peered through the field glasses.

"Crap! By now he's probably realized McCabe brought him out here on a wild goose chase." Romero turned to Davis. "How about it, Officer Davis, do you think you can pick the guy off from here?"

"I've been known to do that, but mostly in a straight across shot from the upper stories of a building. Here, we have to factor in not only the distance, but the velocity of the wind, and it's pretty breezy today," Davis said.

"Let's get on those calculations then, things are starting to look pretty hairy," Romero said.

Davis pulled out his iPhone and scrolled to his dope book, an app he used to determine distances and as his go to guide for firing points. The detectives stood by and watched as he tapped and retapped numbers into his phone.

"Okay, I think I've got it. Let's get this show rolling," Davis said.

Chacon whistled as Davis lifted the latches on the metal case and pulled out his Barrett Lapua M-98, a .338 caliber rifle. "Jee-zus, man. You could kill an elephant with that," he said.

"At least," Davis said. "Of my little weapon arsenal, I rely on this one for distance, although it's a mother to haul around. I'm just hoping we can get the right shot." The men watched in awe as Davis shoved the heavy magazine in and blew a puff of air on the trigger.

As Davis moved toward the ledge of the old building to gauge his shot, Romero put out his arm. "Oh, dammit all to hell!" he said. "Hold up there for a minute." He handed the binoculars back to Martinez. "Am I going crazy or is there some movement in the bushes to the left?"

Martinez shook his head. "Ah, damn...that's McCabe's wife!"

***

Laura slowly peered around the side of the mountain. She could see her husband and Sherman standing in front of the cave. She stood motionless in the brambles, afraid she might be heard. She steadied the gun in her hand and then froze, holding her breath. It was all she could do to keep from passing out.

"You lying sonofabitch," Sherman hollered, pushing McCabe's shoulder. "There's nothing here and you knew it. You're going to pay for this and I'll take care of your wife later." He pointed his weapon at McCabe.

On the other side of the property, the detectives watched as the scene unfolded. "What the hell?" Romero muttered.

The exploding sound shattered the quiet, sending a flock of piñon jays scattering into the air from the nearby junipers. Sherman gripped his shoulder and howled in pain, his weapon dropping to the ground. McCabe ducked to the floor, picked up the gun and pulled Sherman's arm behind him.

"Hey, you're hurting me!" he growled.

McCabe gritted his teeth. "Not as much as I'd like to," he said.

Romero and his men bounded across the field. They grabbed Sherman and wound the flex cuffs tight around his wrists.

McCabe rushed to his wife's side. She burst into tears, barely aware of Tim's arms around her.

"You're shivering, Honey," he said.

"I'm still in shock. I was so afraid he was going to kill you, I didn't know what to do," she said, tears filling her eyes.

McCabe hugged her. "You never cease to amaze me. When we get home, you're going to tell me how you pulled this off, but right now, I just want to hold you."

Laura smiled up at him. "That's fine with me," she said.

McCabe turned to Romero. "What took you so long?"

Romero wiped imaginary sweat from his forehead. "Looks like that sharp-shooting wife of yours took care of business. We were over there across the field ready to go all Clint Eastwood on this guy. Sniper was ready to blow him all to hell."

He turned to Laura. "I have to say, Mrs. M. That was quite a heroic feat you just performed."

McCabe beamed. "In her day, this little lady of mine was a crack shot with a pistol." He planted a kiss on her forehead. "This is one time I'm so happy she never forgot her way around a firearm."

Chacon drove across the field and parked the Chevy next to the Hummer. McCabe pointed Romero to the first aid kit in the compartment near the back door.

"Better patch this guy up. He's not so hurt that we need to wait for an ambulance. It will be faster if we transport him ourselves," said McCabe.

Officer Davis reached for the kit. "Here, let me do it. I've had lots of combat experience patching up the wounded, although I might say they weren't always the bad guys like this one," he said. He knelt on the ground next to Sherman. "This might hurt a little. I'm not going to try to take the bullet out, but at least I'll stop the bleeding until we get you to the hospital and they can patch you up there."

Sherman was silent, not uttering even a grunt as Davis pressed the gauze on his shoulder and taped him up.

McCabe held on to his wife, gently leading her in the direction of the Hummer.

"You guys going to be okay?" Romero said. "One of us can drive you back home."

McCabe shook his head and winked. "My adrenalin's still pumping, but I think we can manage, thanks. I need to get this pretty lady back home and shower her with kisses. I promised her a night out on the town and that's one promise I'm keeping."

Laura smiled and leaned on his shoulder.

Chapter Thirty-Nine

JEMIMAH SPENT PART of her day catching up on writing reports. The file on this case overflowed with a long paper trail, and there was still only one suspect, her father, Jason Hodge. She wondered if this focus on him was political. The present DA was newly elected and intent on establishing a name for himself. So far, according to Rick, he had convinced the department he had a cut and dried case: victim plus suspect plus arrest equals end of story.

Although this situation had struck so close to home and she had to remain objective, Jemimah still had a nagging feeling. Something was amiss and she was determined to sort it all out. Another quick review of the main file resulted in nothing more than magnifying that feeling. She took a bite of the sandwich she hadn't finished for lunch. It was four o'clock.

She decided to leave early to avoid the traffic. Her gas gauge flashed intermittently, warning that only a few miles worth of gas remained in the tank. She figured she could make it to the Highway 14 exit. About ten miles from home, she pulled in next to a gas pump at an Allsup's store, slid her card into the machine, punched the button and inserted the nozzle into the tank.

Feeling the need for a crunchy snack, she wandered into the convenience store and headed for the chip section. While she browsed through the bags of corn chips, she happened to look up and notice the video cameras placed strategically around the store, which were being serviced by a technician in a grey uniform. As he climbed down the ladder, she moved to the left to give him room.

"Excuse me, can I ask you a question?" she said.

"Sure, lady. What can I do for you?" the tech said.

Jemimah craned her neck to look up at him. "Do the video cameras you're working on operate 24-7?"

The tech pulled a replacement battery out of the box and pointed to the lens of the camera. "These are actually activated by motion. Any movement in certain areas inside or out will start them recording," he said.

Jemimah watched as he climbed the ladder. "And would you say that your company has the most convenience stores throughout the Southwest, more than 7-11, say?"

"Yes, I would venture a guess that that's correct. Since we are connected to Texaco, there are probably more Texaco gas cards out there than others. You won't find very many Shell stations on the interstate from California to New Mexico." He looked down the ladder at her. "That's an odd question to ask, if I might add," he said. "You casing the joint?"

Jemimah laughed. "Oh, just curious, I guess, and I had a few minutes to kill while my car filled up. I've always been fascinated by the technology involved. Thank you for the information."

The technician smiled and tipped his hat. "Yes, ma'am. You have a good day."

Deciding on a healthier snack than salt-laden chips, Jemimah reached for a packet of almonds, paid the cashier and headed out to her car. The pump registered full and she replaced the nozzle and closed the lid on the gas cap. She pulled into her driveway fifteen minutes later. "Ah, home sweet home," she said, as she watched her dog bolt out of the porch to greet her. Romero's vehicle was parked next to the barn. She smiled and hoped dinner would already be on the table. Her feet were killing her.

Romero greeted her at the door with a long kiss.

"Wow," she said, returning the kiss. "Are you happy to see me or is that a revolver in your pocket," she quipped.

He laughed. "A little of both." He led her to the couch and waited while she slipped off her shoes and reclined back. "Relax for a minute. I cooked up a batch of grilled chicken and veggies. Thought we could take a break from the spicy hot stuff."

"Smells yummy," she said.

He returned to the kitchen, poured them both a margarita, handed Jemimah a glass and sat beside her. "I think this will help recharge our spirits," he said.

Jemimah took a salty sip and set the glass down on the table. "I was wondering where you had gone off to this afternoon. Last I heard you had picked Tim up at the airport and were dropping him off. I expected to beat you home," she said.

Romero leaned back and stretched. "That's how my afternoon started off, then all hell broke loose."

Her eyes widened. "Oh my God, what happened?" He related the entire adventure involving the McCabes, their being kidnapped and Laura's heroic efforts in rescuing her husband.

When he was finished Jemimah clapped her hands. "Oh, go Laura! I've always known there was a real titan behind that quiet demeanor of hers. I can just picture her aiming that pistol at the bad guy."

Romero chuckled. "Yes, it was quite a sight to see that tiny woman in action. McCabe couldn't hardly contain himself."

After a quiet dinner, the couple retired to the bedroom. The lights were dimmed, the king-sized bed was covered with rose petals, and a bottle of bubbly.

"Oh, you," she said, as he reached out for her.

Chapter Forty

J EMIMAH WAS RECHARGED from spending the Memorial Day holiday eating junk food and watching chick flicks, which Romero said he disliked but seemed to enjoy. Seated on a lawn chair on the terrace outside the French doors from her downtown office in the early morning quiet of that Wednesday, she took a deep breath and looked out across San Francisco Street. She could see all the way to the historic La Fonda Hotel and the Basilica of St. Francis Cathedral. To her left across from the central plaza park was the Palace of the Governors where Native American craftsmen milled around, waiting to stick their hand in a large pottery jar to pick a number that would assure them a space to sell their wares under the historic portal on that day.

She sipped on the cream-drizzled iced latte and reviewed the previous weekend's events in her mind. She had gone through the case file thoroughly, even a second time. There were moments when the thought entered her mind of the likelihood that her father had actually committed the murder. After all, he was acquainted with the victim, albeit through the bizarre circumstances of being involved with his ex-wife. Jemimah didn't know what to do with these thoughts. It was her job to be objective and there was no getting around it. Once again she wondered if she might be in denial about that possibility. Yet throughout her career as a psychologist, she prided herself on being a good judge of character, even though this suspect was a close relative.

Just as she was getting ready to go back into to her office and start her day, Jemimah decided to revisit her info on the victim's ex-wife and the fiancée. She thought she just might be ignoring the obvious. These two women could be holding the key to the solution of this mystery. On the one hand, everyone Jemimah spoke to about Brigid, her father's fourth wife, including the sister wives, felt she was genuine and held no animosity toward her ex-husband, Lawrence Tanner. Not so true about her feelings toward the other women, and lack of such for his fiancée.

On the other hand, an equal number of individuals seemed to think Eliza Simpson was perfect. She participated in church activities, volunteered for major causes, made herself available to anyone in need. They had nothing but praise for this woman.

Jemimah tapped her pen on the desk and pulled out the interview file from the desk drawer. She rifled through her notes looking for something the Simpson woman had nonchalantly interjected into their conversation. Feeling sympathetic toward the woman, Jemimah inquired if there was someone Eliza could turn to for grief counseling when she returned to Provo, she mentioned the bishop and a Doctor Blake Parker.

She sat at her desk and booted up her laptop. She found a psychiatrist by that name who practiced at a clinic on the outskirts of Provo. She Googled for information on him and was surprised to learn that in addition to being a practicing psychiatrist with an enviable practice, he was also an outspoken critic who had left the Mormon Church some years before. Jemimah placed an early morning call to the clinic in Moab, Utah. Dr. Parker's secretary put her call through.

Jemimah introduced herself, mentioned her credentials and explained that she was working on a case involving a woman named Eliza Simpson as a witness. "I'm looking to fill in a few gaps, and she casually mentioned that she knew you," she said. "Do you have a moment, and if you don't mind I'd like to ask a few questions?"

Dr. Parker put her on hold while he checked his patient schedule. He returned to the call a minute later. "I can give you about thirty minutes, then I have a patient coming in."

"I'll try to make this short," Jemimah said. "Can you give me some background on Miss Simpson?"

"Wow, this is going back in time a few years. I first met her when she was sixteen. Her parents brought her to see me because she had been having episodes of uncontrollable anger," he said.

"What kind of episodes, if you recall," Jemimah said.

"The usual teen-aged acting up, which included screaming, accusatory remarks, extreme and intense self-hatred, coupled with completely self-absorbed narcissistic tendencies which included blowing small problems out of proportion," he said.

As he talked on, Jemimah scribbled notes on a tablet. "How long was she your patient, Doctor?"

"On and off for about three years, and then she asked to be released from my care. She had enrolled at Brigham Young University and hoped to pursue a degree."

"That would make her around nineteen?" Jemimah said.

"Yes. Over time I had determined that for the most part, much of her erratic conduct was her way of getting back at her parents, who were extremely controlling and manipulative. I released her and she promised to follow up at least once every six months."

"And did she?" Jemimah said.

"Actually no, and I wasn't surprised," he said.

"As a psychologist myself, I'm aware that I have to be cautious about certain inquiries due to the inherent doctor/patient relationship. But I would like to ask if you ever saw her again?" Jemimah asked.

He paused and then chuckled. "That doctor/patient

relationship doesn't apply any longer, particularly since I married her and had a completely different set of circumstances to relate to. I'm speaking as a spouse, not a doctor. There is also case law on the books in this state regarding that."

Jemimah felt her eyebrows raise. "I see."

Sensing her reaction, he continued. "It's not what you think. She had matured as an adult, and had not been my patient for a number of years since she reached maturity and there was nothing unethical about our dating. Some years after she graduated from BYU with her Master's, we became colleagues. She was working for a non-profit and I was on the board. Long story short, the marriage didn't last long."

"Might I ask the reason?"

"Oh, that's a horse of another color," he laughed. "Everything I treated her for as a teenager came back like a hurricane."

"By that I assume you mean she returned to her early behavior?" Jemimah said.

"In essence, yes. She started going off the deep end for every little thing, blowing minor incidents way out of proportion. We eventually separated but stayed in contact with each other, and at some point after being apart for several months, Eliza made overtures about reconciling. But before I was willing to entertain that possibility, I insisted she see a colleague of mine to resolve some of her issues."

"Did she do that?" Jemimah asked.

"She saw Dr. Karen White for a few visits, but I noticed her demeanor continued to be erratic and unpredictable, so I eventually filed for divorce," he said.

"What was her reaction to that, if I might ask?"

He sighed audibly. "The main thing she was annoyed about was that our prenup precluded her from walking away with nothing more than a cash settlement, but it was a substantial one and I'm sure she managed quite well."

Jemimah glanced at the time. "Did you see her after that?"

"No, but I do know that Dr. White was summoned to the hospital at one point to treat her for a psychological incident."

"How long ago was that, if you recall?" Jemimah asked.

"Maybe five years. Eliza was in her late twenties."

"And did you discuss her case with Dr. White?"

"No, I did not, but if I had, in that instance it would be unethical for me to repeat," he said.

"I understand. You said you had additional information about Eliza's mental condition. Where would that have come from?" Jemimah said.

"From my own experience. I knew when her dark moods hit, she was a handful to deal with. Shortly after we parted, I was on call in the psych ward of the hospital, and I discussed her chart with the attending physician. This was during the period where we had considered reconciling, and I wanted to be sure what was going on with her. The doctor indicated she was prescribed a number of medications when she was dismissed," he said.

"Was there a diagnosis indicated on her chart?"

"The notes reflected that she was experiencing severe anxiety, coupled with a heightened belief that everyone was out to get her. What might have brought this paranoia on was a combination of alcohol and meds, which created a unique reaction," he said.

"Doctor, one last question. As a psychiatrist yourself, can you share an opinion of what your diagnosis would be if you were presented with a client who exhibited similar characteristics as those of Eliza Simpson," Jemimah said.

"Of course, as a licensed practitioner, you are aware of the exceptions to confidentiality for mental care providers?" he asked. "We know it as the Dangerous Patient Exception, where a therapist can disclose information if a patient is capable of doing harm to another person."

"Yes," Jemimah said. "I am."

"For that reason, I'm going to go out on a limb here because of the case law that addresses that issue. I don't have it front of me, so I'll give you my personal opinion of Eliza's condition. I believe she is an incurable sociopath who suffers from delusions of grandeur, and is completely self-absorbed and narcissistic. I'm not sure she ever brought her anger issues under control, but as you probably know from your own practice, a sociopath is able to give everyone the impression that they are perfect in every way, while underneath the surface, a volcano waits to erupt if the right circumstances present themselves."

"Do you think she would ever be capable of harming another person?" Jemimah said.

"If she hasn't changed much over the years and her anger has been stifled and allowed to build without a safe outlet, and if circumstances were in place that she couldn't handle like a normal person, I would definitely say that she might be capable of a major outburst which could result in harm to someone who she feels has gotten in her way. I can't say that for sure, but that would be my educated guess."

Jemimah thanked him for his time and then hung up. She wondered if his educated guess might be right on target. She put in a call to Tim McCabe and asked him to see if he could find any additional info on Eliza Simpson's travels over the previous two months by mapping a route from Utah to New Mexico and checking for any gas card charges.

Chapter Forty-One

———

TIM MCCABE TOOK the steps two at a time and walked down the long hallway to Jemimah's office. Katie was gazing intently at her computer when he strolled in. She looked up to greet him.

"Dr. Hodge is out of the office, Tim. Can I help you with anything?" Katie said. "You can wait if you like. She should be in momentarily, and help yourself to a cup of coffee. Just finished brewing."

"Thank you, don't mind if I do." He headed for the kitchen, filled a mug, and on his way back to the conference room slipped into the chair next to Katie. He took a sip of coffee and glanced at her computer screen. "What's that you're looking at, Katie?"

She spun her chair to face him. "Oh, every so often I like to check out the Google Earth live feed of downtown Santa Fe." She pointed to the screen. "See, there's the Palace of the Governors and the park in the center of the Plaza. You can see people milling around, and even Roque's fajita truck and a line of customers waiting to be served," she said.

McCabe fished his reading glasses from his shirt pocket and leaned into the monitor. "I'm not too Internet savvy, Katie, but are these Googly cameras just in Santa Fe or are they out on the highways, too?"

Katie laughed. "They're all over the place. That's why they call it Google Earth. I took an Internet course last year at the community college on this subject because it is so intriguing."

"Explain it to me in plain language, Katie. You're talking to someone who doesn't know much more about computers than accessing email," he said, "and I don't always get that right."

"I'll do my best, Tim. Live highway camera feeds are available to anyone these days. You just have to log on to Google Street View. You see this window here that says 'search'? Well you just type in the area you want to view and Google brings it up. Law enforcement can tap into the Department of Transportation servers, to get additional footage and history not available to the public. Then there are businesses who have security cameras which cover not only their parking lots, but also face the road," she explained.

"Whew, that's amazing. So do you know if these areas are accessible for a time prior to the present?" he said.

"Pretty sure. As I understand it, the images are recorded on hard drives, which means they are stored. I'm sure a particular area can be accessed through the right channels."

McCabe jumped to his feet. "Katie, you just opened up a whole new world for me. It looks like I won't need to see Dr. Hodge." He leaned down and kissed the top of her head, thanked her and headed for the door. The education he just received from Katie was going to help him gather the information on tracking Eliza Simpson's movements. He bounded down the steps, and walked down San Francisco Street to the parking garage to the underground level to retrieve his vehicle.

Within moments he was sitting in the front seat, having a conversation on his cell phone with auto rental companies based at the Albuquerque airport. After dead ends from the first two companies, on the third try McCabe would find that indeed there was another car rental charged to an E. Simpson from several weeks before the current rental. He requested the company send copies to Romero's fax of the rental agreement and the accompanying identifiers, which included her driver's license and Social Security number. He headed for the substation, where he intended to retrieve the documents and compare the signature to the ones in the file which reflected the most recent rental record.

That morning, knowing Jemimah would be interested, Detective Romero had obtained a warrant allowing the gas credit card company to release their records regarding any charges Eliza Simpson might have made for the period in question. By the time McCabe arrived at the substation, Clarissa had already printed copies out for him to peruse. He made a quick note of the places she had charged gas, and then slipped them into his file. He still had a few more tasks to complete before he could sit down and put things in order to present his findings to his colleagues.

Romero had also cleared the way for the convenience stores to release security footage for several days leading up to and after the time in question. The security manager for the Allsup's stores burned DVDs as requested and also provided a thumb drive. McCabe picked them up and drove to the main office where he logged all the information into evidence and was provided with duplicates, which he packaged up and delivered to Jemimah's office.

On his way to lunch, McCabe texted both Jemimah and Detective Romero. "Mission accomplished."

Chapter Forty-Two

J EMIMAH COULD HARDLY contain herself as she ripped open
the packet McCabe left for her, from which she pulled a set
of DVDs. Katie sat down in front of her computer and inserted
one into the slot.

"Okay, Boss, here we go. We're lucky my computer is so
outdated that it still has a DVD drive." She clicked her mouse
on the arrow to start the first video, and slid a tablet closer to
take notes. She Googled Mapquest to locate the shortest routes
from Utah to New Mexico.

Surprisingly the footage on the security videos covering
a two week period was of good quality, compared to those
in previous cases. They scrolled slowly through hundreds of
black and white images of both employees and clientele of the
Allsup's stores along the highways coming into New Mexico
from Colorado.

When footage of a lone woman approaching the
convenience store in Redlands, Colorado popped up, Katie
froze the image and noted the date and time. Jemimah leaned
closer to the screen and had Katie do a short rewind. They
watched as the vehicle pulled into the station and up to the
pump. The woman stepped out onto the driveway, inserted her

card into the machine and gassed up. She entered the store, went into the bathroom, exited and browsed through the coolers against the back wall. At the checkout counter she paid the clerk in cash for a bottle of water, Diet Coke and a deep fried bean burrito.

As the customer stood at the checkout stand, Katie zoomed in for a close-up, printed out a photo and handed it to Jemimah. Jemimah put on her reading glasses and took a careful look.

"That's her. That's Eliza Simpson! Katie, this proves without a doubt that she was in the area right around the time of the murder," Jemimah said. They continued to track the video as the woman exited the store and another camera captured her image as she entered her vehicle, buckled up and pulled out onto the highway. Katie again froze the image as the video captured the license plate number of the car, which matched the information from the rental company provided by McCabe. The time stamp on the video and the receipt copy for her gas purchase matched. Jemimah was elated.

Other gas receipts provided by Texaco added additional information. They followed a direct route from Provo through a small part of Colorado, into Farmington, New Mexico and then on to Albuquerque and finally at Santa Fe.

"She doesn't appear to be in any hurry or even aware that she might be on camera," Katie said. "In addition, she doesn't purchase gas every time she stops at a convenience store, just to stretch, buy a soda and use the bathroom facilities."

When they were finished, Jemimah gathered the DVDs and her notes and placed them in the case folder, stuffed them in her briefcase and thanked Katie for her help.

"This has been invaluable, Katie. Take the rest of the day off. I need to spend some time pulling this all together," she said. "Maybe tonight, if Rick is stuck at work again, which seems to be the case lately."

Katie giggled and pointed to the clock on the wall. It was six o'clock. "We're already into overtime, Boss."

Jemimah blushed. "Well, sleep in and come in late

tomorrow morning instead."

On her way home Jemimah tapped her phone and listened to a message from Romero. He had a dinner meeting with Sheriff Medrano and the County Commissioners to beg for funding to hire additional officers. She knew how those meetings went, sometimes pointless, sometimes fruitful, and she also knew it would be way past her bedtime when he returned home.

On the bright side, this would provide an opportunity for her to review the case file and prepare her notes for an impromptu meeting with him and McCabe. She speed dialed the pizza place in Cerrillos and picked up her dinner fifteen minutes later. Arriving home, she was greeted at the door by Gato, who purred noisily and plopped a dead mouse at her feet. Not to be outdone by the cat, Molly was whirling around like a dervish trying to get her attention.

Chapter Forty-Three

B Y THE TIME Jemimah awoke the next morning, Rick had already headed for another early meeting with the Sheriff, after which they would meet at the substation. She grabbed a quick breakfast of leftover pizza and strong coffee, showered, dressed and headed to the substation. As she pulled into the parking lot, Tim McCabe was alarming his vehicle. He walked over to embrace her and they entered the satellite office together. Romero was standing over Clarissa and retrieving messages from the previous day.

"Look at this pretty lady I found out in the parking lot," McCabe chuckled.

Romero put his arms around Jemimah and gave her a quick peck on the lips. "Good morning, Sunshine," he said. "You were sleeping like a log when I came in last night, and I didn't want to disturb your beauty sleep this morning."

A big smile crossed Jemimah's face. "Well at least you two got my message about getting together this morning. I wasn't sure if I was going to be conducting this review by myself."

Romero motioned them toward the conference room. "We must be having a déjà vu day. I listened to Jemimah's message, I was about to call you two, thinking it was about time we sat down and compared notes on this case. Better late than never."

"Great minds think alike, Rick," said McCabe. Both he and Jemimah set their case files on the table in the conference room, as Detective Romero slid his file in front of him. Clarissa had set out a carafe of coffee, along with an assortment of baked goods.

"Leave it to Clarissa to provide another opportunity to expand my waistline," McCabe said, looking over the plateful of sweets.

Jemimah poured a round of coffee into ceramic mugs. She tore the end off a Stevia packet, poured it and some cream into the cup and thoughtfully stirred. She took a long sip, relishing the creamy texture. McCabe followed suit.

Jemimah passed each of them a copy of a memo. "This has turned out to be a very complex case. I've delineated what we have so far. To paraphrase, we have a victim who was killed out in the woods and then covered with a sleeping bag. What would that indicate?" she said.

Romero swirled a shot of cream into his mug and tapped the spoon on the edge. "That maybe our killer was close to the victim and couldn't stand the sight of seeing him dead? Maybe some act of remorse and concern that wild animals would soon encounter a dead body lying out in their midst? Most victims are killed by someone they know, and I'm not sure this isn't any different," he said. "Jason Hodge, Eliza Simpson and Brigid Hodge all knew him, and perhaps someone else we are unaware of."

"I agree," Jemimah said. "I believe I've conducted as many interviews as there are to be had, even exploring the jealousy angle. The victim, Lawrence Tanner, was the ex-husband of Brigid Tanner, the most recent sister wife in the Hodge group. He was a practicing Mormon, not a member of the FLDS, so therefore not a polygamist, and had strong feelings on that subject. Apparently his ex-wife, Brigid, was open to becoming another one of the sister wives in the Hodge group, and was introduced as a prospect sometime after her divorce from the victim became final, or maybe even before."

McCabe reached for a cinnamon roll and thoughtfully pulled off a section with his fingers. "Sounds like we're going to need a score card to keep track of all the players," he said. "There's more individuals involved in this crime than usual."

Jemimah took a sip of coffee and then set the mug down to her left. "What has me baffled is Hodge's relationship with Brigid Tanner. From what I've gleaned in the interviews, I'm thinking that she was favored in his eyes, so much that he missed many of the prescheduled nights with the other three wives," she said. "And bear with me, I'm having a little difficulty referring to the suspect as 'my father.'"

"Hodge works for me," said McCabe. Romero nodded.

"As a psychologist, it's very easy for me to make judgment calls, but this is a difficult one. When I read between the lines on the interviews with these women, there was an underlying current I don't think any of them was aware of. It was apparent to me that they really didn't like Brigid, the new kid on the block, and that each of them was repressing her true feelings so as not to make waves and provoke the ire of their husband.

"And when Brigid was introduced into their midst as a fourth prospect, it threw them all for a loop. At first, they all tried to get along, and then somewhere along the line, Brigid began making more demands on the husband. I think it irritated the wives that all of a sudden he now had many excuses for not spending their assigned nights together."

McCabe raised his eyebrows. "Did they actually have a calendar with the dates the husband was to spend the night with them?"

"Oh, yes, it's a common practice in these situations. That way one of the wives couldn't plan an event that infringed on someone else's allotted time," Jemimah said. "Of course, birthdays and anniversaries were exceptions and the calendar was adjusted to reflect those dates. Brigid also mentioned that her ex-husband, the victim, was insistent on getting back together even though they had both moved on. I'm sure she harbored some anger in that regard, even if she didn't express such."

Romero refilled his cup and returned to the table. "Are you considering Brigid Tanner as a suspect because she might have killed her ex-husband to get him out of the way?"

Jemimah shook her head. "Other than a couple of run-ins with her ex and the stress he created by his demands of reconciliation on her, it didn't appear to me that she had a strong enough motive. When the marriage broke up, she had moved on with her life and assumed the victim had also. Now, here's where it gets tricky.

"I do believe our killer must have had a connection to the victim. Let's assume that the sleeping bag wasn't anywhere near the victim until after the altercation, or lack of, that led to the homicide. There was no indication that he was getting ready to camp out and was probably still hiking around the nearby trails."

Chapter Forty-Four

ROMERO PUSHED HIS chair back and stood up to stretch. "Where are you going with this, Jem? I assume the case is moving in a different direction with the information we've gathered about Simpson being in the area before she said she was," he said.

"Exactly. That was my next statement. What if Eliza Simpson shot him, whether by intent or by accident, and then covered him with the sleeping bag because she couldn't stand to see the body. Death by homicide is not pretty. She would have been looking at a gruesome sight and in a moment of panic, let's say she ran back to the car, retrieved the sleeping bag from the trunk, and returned to the scene and covered him," Jemimah said.

Romero pulled a packet from his file. "If you look at the crime scene photos, the bag wasn't just thrown over the body. See, it was spread over him as in making a bed. And there wasn't much blood evidence, indicating the victim wasn't in a supine position on the ground when he was killed," Romero said.

Jemimah nodded. "In our initial interview, Eliza Simpson had an awful lot to say about Brigid Tanner, and none of it nice.

In fact, she insinuated that Brigid had been excommunicated from the religion because of the divorce and it didn't seem to bother her at all.

"But it did appear to bother Tanner. He was well respected in the Mormon community, and he felt that the divorce had placed a black checkmark on his reputation, so he tried several times to convince his ex-wife to return to him and that all would be forgiven. Eventually, and probably because she had already moved in with Hodge, he gave up and entered into a relationship with Eliza Simpson, the woman who is now his fiancée."

Romero flipped through his notes. "Yes, I spoke with her by phone shortly after the body was identified, and then she showed up at my office a few days later. I think you have a copy of my report," he said.

"Along this same vein," Jemimah continued, "it occurred to me that based on some of the remarks Simpson made in our interview, it started me thinking she might have actually been in Santa Fe more recently than she said. According to her statement, after she learned of her boyfriend's death, she immediately flew into Albuquerque, rented a car, and came directly to see Rick at his office. In our interview, she mentioned attending a Santa Fe Symphony presentation that same evening to calm her nerves.

"Now, get this. Talk about coincidence. I happened to be at home sitting on the couch browsing through the Symphony catalog we periodically receive in the mail, and before I tossed it, I noticed that the particular presentation Simpson claims to have attended that evening, had actually occurred four or five days before," Jemimah said.

"I checked with the ticket seller at the Lensic Performing Center to see if perhaps the concert had been repeated, and they said it had not."

McCabe whistled. "So that's what prompted our looking into the possibility she might have been in the area around the same time as the victim?"

Jemimah pushed a stray hair from her forehead. "Yes, and there's more. When she showed me her driver's license, I noticed that the card beneath it was a Texaco card. McCabe checked with the company to see what gas purchases she might have made within two weeks prior to the discovery of the victim's body, and those are indicated in the memo. Oh, and another thing. Simpson said she was a widow, but I couldn't find anything to prove that statement was true. If it was and she indeed is our killer here, someone might have to investigate how that husband died. Anyway, that was a curiosity to me and I did a little checking, but it led nowhere."

"We also assumed she's been driving a rental while in town and using the same gas card, and we obtained copies of those recent charges also," said McCabe.

Romero paced around the table. "What did you discover from the videotapes provided by Allsup's?" he asked.

Jemimah reviewed what she and Katie had seen and showed them a copy of the photo they printed out. Romero confirmed it was Eliza Simpson.

"Getting back to my interviews with Simpson, I sensed a bit of antagonism on her part toward Brigid Tanner, but it is probably misdirected. Many times in relationships where there is an ex-partner, the new partner might feel inadequate or left out if there is unintentional or subconscious mention of the ex, good or bad," Jemimah said. "And Simpson was already aware that the victim had made overtures in the past about getting back with the ex-wife. What she might not have been sure of was Brigid Tanner's thoughts on this."

McCabe's chair scraped the floor as he leaned back. "If that's the case, the ex-wife could also have been a victim if our killer decided to do her in instead? That might have alleviated the problem if she saw the ex as a threat. Is that what you're saying?"

"Not in so many words, but that's a good point. My interviews with the other wives didn't produce anything suspicious. I found the four of them to be genuine, albeit each somewhat concerned about themselves more than each other. Along with my birth mother, two of the women have been with him for a long time and produced a number of children with him. For the most part, it appeared that although not a doting father, Hodge was a constant part of their lives and participated in the usual fatherly things expected of a man in his position.

"From each of them I learned that he hadn't been such a terrible person after all. In my interview with Byron Mills, he painted a picture of family togetherness and harmony.

"And yes, I picked up that there was a fair amount of jealousy aimed at the new wife, Brigid, but it was well suppressed, none of them willing to admit to that fact. The sisterly love aspect of their relationship was a bit overplayed, in my opinion.

"Getting back to Eliza Simpson and reading between the lines again, I could see that she hadn't been truly grief-stricken by her fiancé's death. I suspect the tearful act she presented was for our benefit. She never once asked how or why Tanner had been killed. Curious, don't you think?"

Romero looked up as Clarissa tapped on the door. "Yes, Clarissa, what is it?"

Clarissa handed him two sheets of paper. "Detective Chacon's evidence tech just faxed this over to you."

Romero fanned the papers and looked over at Jemimah and McCabe. "Wow, more fodder for the fire."

Chapter Forty-Five

J EMIMAH LOOKED UP at her husband. "What is it, Rick? Don't keep us in suspense," she said.

"First let me give you a quick background. The other day while I was waiting for my meeting to resume, I thumbed through the file and pulled the list of calls made by the victim. I noticed there were a number of calls made to and from his phone after he arrived in Santa Fe, and I had Clarissa put in a call to the service provider to see where some of those calls originated," Romero said.

"Don't tell me...some of them originated in Santa Fe," Jemimah said.

"Yep, a week before the body was discovered, some of the calls bounced off the towers between Albuquerque, Espanola and Santa Fe. I had Detective Chacon and one of the techs triangulate the information from both their cell phones and according to this, they were able to determine that indeed the calls originating from Eliza Simpson's phone were made locally," he said. "But, just because she appears to have been in town during that time doesn't mean she killed him. She might just have been insanely jealous and followed him to see if he was being unfaithful."

Jemimah sat back in her chair. "Shades of *Law and Order,* my favorite TV show. Between this new information, the gasoline charges and the video, evidence doesn't get any better than that."

Romero jotted a note in his tablet. "It appears that the next step is to present our findings to the District Attorney, and also to Hodge's attorney as a courtesy. Then we should give it another once-over, rule out the unimportant and insignificant, and then request a warrant be issued for her arrest."

McCabe refilled his coffee mug. "The manner of death, the very violence of it, suggests that whoever shot Tanner had reason to hate him a great deal. I don't think we've proven that Hodge had a clear motive. He probably didn't like the guy, but he doesn't strike me as the type of person that was going to stalk a victim, shoot him, and then leave him for dead," he said, "especially so close to his own property."

"So, Rick, are you also convinced it was someone else other than Hodge?" Jemimah said.

"It sure as heck looks that way. In the first place, I don't think initially there was enough evidence to connect him to the crime, other than the murder weapon being found in one of the outbuildings on his property. That's just way too convenient. We all know crimes don't get solved that easily," Romero said. "Only an inexperienced criminal would believe that planting the murder weapon was going to assure a conviction and move the suspicion away from themselves. Unfortunately it was all we had at the time."

He looked at his watch. "We need to wrap this up, guys. I've got Medrano on my ass about this case and everything else. My detectives are finally back on the force after a few grueling weeks without them at FBI Academy, so I have to bring them up to date, reassign some of our current case load and get them moving."

Jemimah touched his arm. "Rick, I have another request to put this all in the right sequence, and I need you to do something for me," she said.

He grinned. "Sure, Sweetie. Does it involve lots of hugging and kissing?"

She playfully pushed him away. "No, silly. This is serious."

McCabe chuckled. "*Bueno*, you two. Get a room, why don't you?"

Romero straightened his back. "All right, let me put on my serious face. What do you need, Doctor Hodge?"

"To save me having to go through the usual channels for permission, would you mind getting me a copy of any test results the lab might have conducted on the substances found on the victim's shoes? Maybe we can include Eliza Simpson's shoes on that warrant request," she said.

"Will do," he said.

McCabe stood. "Meeting adjourned, I presume?"

"Regarding this case, yes," Romero said. "But I need your input on another matter I've been spinning my wheels on, Tim. Shouldn't take too long." He leaned over to Jemimah and bussed her on the cheek. "See you tonight."

After Jemimah left the office, McCabe turned to Detective Romero. "I could see the wheels churning in Jemimah's pretty head. She's about pulled this case together," he said.

"Yeah, I didn't marry her just for her beauty." Romero quipped.

Jemimah headed into Santa Fe to run errands and do some grocery shopping. On her return trip, she missed the five o'clock traffic down Highway 14. Romero's cruiser and McCabe's Hummer were still parked in front of the satellite office. It would give her time to leisurely fix dinner, relax and take a breather. She sighed with relief as she pulled into her driveway.

After picking up the mail and greeting an energized Molly dog, she entered the back porch and unlocked the kitchen door. She reset the alarm, slipped her bag off her shoulder and set it on the hassock. Black pumps were next, followed by her jacket. She flicked on the TV as she headed toward the counter to browse through the mail, tossing about three quarters of it into the trash. She grabbed a cold beer from the fridge and plopped herself on the couch. She leaned back into the soft cushions. Molly looked up and tilted her head as she heard a long sigh.

Jemimah must have dozed off, as the next thing she heard was Molly barking her head off, scratching at the living room window. She smiled as she watched Romero park his cruiser and come up the walk. It reminded her of the first time he picked her up for a dinner date. She had felt the chemistry between them early on, but chose to deny it until she could no longer hide her feelings. He came through the door and she ran up to him and nestled close, her head against his shoulder. He was warm and strong, and she loved him.

He held her at arm's length. "Now that's the kind of greeting every guy should have. What's the occasion?"

She kissed him passionately. "The occasion is that I love you and if we don't get this honeymoon on the road soon, I'm going to go batty. What do you have to say to that, Detective?"

He wrapped his arms around her neck and pulled her closer. "Just this." He spun her around and led her into the bedroom.

Chapter Forty-Six

━━━━◆━━━━

Tʜᴇ ɴᴇxᴛ ᴍᴏʀɴɪɴɢ as McCabe was leaving home, his cell phone pinged. It was Detective Romero.

"Yeah, Rick. What's up?"

"Tim, meet me at the Lamplighter Hotel on Cerrillos Road. ETA about fifteen minutes. Wait for me in the parking lot. I'll explain when I get there," Romero said.

McCabe arrived first, pulled the Hummer into a parking space under a tree and waited a few minutes for Detective Romero to arrive. The detective parked in the adjoining space and both alighted their vehicles. McCabe pushed the alarm pod on his keychain and walked over to Romero's side.

"I take it we've got a job to do here, Rick? I'm surprised this place is still standing. I read somewhere it was one of the first motels built in the 1950s," he said. "At the time, this was the southern outskirts of Santa Fe, the boonies."

"Nothing seems to change in this part of town." Romero thumbed toward the motel entrance. "I've been waiting for this moment. Let's go get our murderer."

They walked across the parking lot, down the sidewalk leading to the hotel lobby. The sliding glass doors were decorated with a cactus motif painted in garish shades of green. The lobby was furnished with clunky wagon-wheel furniture set on multi-colored woven rugs with frayed edges.

Romero approached the desk clerk and asked for Eliza Simpson's room number. The clerk keyed in the name on his keyboard and pulled up a screen on his computer.

"Hmmm. It looks like she's already checked out," he said.

"How long ago was that?" Romero said.

The clerk scrolled down the screen. "Not very long, maybe fifteen minutes or so. I believe she mentioned she was going over to the Hertz desk and turn her car in, and then take the shuttle to the airport. She might still be at the rental counter." He pointed them in a direction to the left of the entrance.

"Damn," Romero said. "Looks like we just missed her."

They rounded the corner and walked across the atrium where the car rental kiosk was located. Romero flashed his credentials to the young woman monitoring the desk. She checked her files and informed them the car in question had already been checked in. He instructed her to put a hold on the vehicle until he could make arrangements for it to be picked up and processed.

Romero looked up at the clock on the wall and the name tag on the counter. "Brenda, can you tell me what time the shuttle picks up for the airport?"

She smiled sweetly at him. "It should be here in about ten minutes, more or less," she said.

McCabe leaned toward her. "Are they usually on time?"

She nodded. "They pick up at several hotels. We're the last on the schedule, so depending on how many passengers are waiting, they usually show up within a few minutes of the time listed on their flyer," she said.

She directed them to the passenger waiting area.

"Come on, McCabe. With any luck they haven't picked up yet," Romero said as they rushed outside.

McCabe spotted a woman sitting on a bench, thumbing through a magazine. "Is that her, Rick?"

"It damn sure is."

Eliza Simpson looked up with a surprised look on her face. She hesitated then reached up to smooth her hair. "Detective Romero. Did you forget something?"

"Miss Simpson, we'd like a word with you," he said.

She glanced at her watch. "I don't see how I can help you, but make it quick. I have a flight to catch."

"You'll have to postpone that flight," McCabe said.

She stood abruptly. "Excuse me? I'll do no such thing. I have to be back on the job tomorrow morning," she said.

"Miss Simpson, we'd like to have that conversation down town. You can make other travel arrangements when we're done," Romero said.

She looked first at McCabe then at Romero. "Why is this necessary, Detective. I've told you everything I know. Surely you need to place your focus on the main suspect in this case."

As they stood there, the shuttle drove up and she reached for her bag as the door of the bus swung open. She turned to head in that direction.

Romero blocked her path. "Miss Simpson. We can do this quietly without a scene, or I can handcuff you right here and drag you screaming and hollering to our patrol car. Your choice."

She straightened her back and tossed her head. "All right, but you're going to have to arrange transportation for me to catch the next flight. I'm not losing my job over your insistence to continue to harass me."

Romero nodded. "If it comes to that, I'll see what we can do." He motioned to McCabe who reached over for her luggage and wheeled it behind them as they headed for Romero's cruiser. He opened the back passenger side and directed her in. McCabe left his car in the lot and slid into the front seat of Romero's vehicle.

Romero pulled out onto the road and headed south toward Highway 599. He turned into the Santa Fe County Detention Facility.

Eliza Simpson had been silent the entire fifteen minute

drive to the County Jail complex. Once there, she was taken to an interrogation room. Detective Romero reached into his wallet and pulled out a card, from which he read Simpson her Miranda rights.

"Miss Simpson, do you understand that you have the right to remain silent. Anything you say can be used against you. You have the right to an attorney. If you cannot afford one, one will be appointed to you by the court. With these rights in mind, are you still willing to talk with me about the charges against you?"

Eliza Simpson responded with an indignant scowl on her face. "Yes, I understand my rights, and no, I don't want or need an attorney."

She then sat down on one side of a small table. McCabe and Romero sat on the other. Her hands clasped tightly in front of her, she glared across the table at Romero.

"All right, Detective. Let's get this over with. What is this about? I don't want to miss the next shuttle. I'm cutting it close as it is," she said.

"Miss Simpson, you are here because we have a suspicion that you might be responsible for the homicide of Lawrence Tanner."

"That's crazy. I did no such thing," she said.

"Let me repeat that you are entitled to have an attorney present, Miss Simpson."

"And I will repeat again that I don't need an attorney. I haven't done anything. I just want to get this over with and get out of here."

"Very well," Romero said. He flipped opened the file on the table in front of him. "I'm going to ask you a few questions related to the death of Lawrence Tanner. I would like for you to think long and hard about your answers," Romero said.

She shrugged her left shoulder and turned her head. "I don't have to think at all. I've told you everything I know, which is nothing. I came here to identify the body and make funeral arrangements. That's it," she said. "I don't understand why you continue to harass me. I can assure you I will lodge a complaint with your supervisors when this is over."

Ignoring her remark, Romero pulled a sheaf of papers from the file. "Do you happen to have a Texaco gasoline card, Miss Simpson?"

Her eyes widened. "What does that have to do with anything?"

"Just answer the question, please," he said.

"Yes, I have several gas cards. There might be a Texaco one in there."

"Do you have them in your possession, and if so, may I see them?" Romero said.

Simpson reached into her purse and pulled out a stack of credit cards. A Texaco credit card was in one of the flaps. She pushed it toward Romero, who made a note of the numbers and handed it back to her.

"Now, Miss Simpson, have you ever been in the Santa Fe area, prior to the time you came here after being notified of Mr. Tanner's death?" Romero said.

"No, I have not." She repeated the information she had previously given in interviews.

Romero noted her timeline of events contained several flaws. She claimed to have not left Utah until after she hadn't heard from her fiancé and received the call from the bishop. Yet her gas card showed not only cash withdrawals, but transactions on two different occasions in Colorado and New Mexico a week or more days prior to her showing up at Romero's office. To that she insisted there must be an error and that she had not departed from Utah until the day after she received the news of Tanner's demise.

Romero could sense the walls going up. He reached for his file. "We're going to take a little break here, Miss Simpson. It will give you time to gather your thoughts," he said. "I'll have some coffee brought in."

Eliza Simpson frowned at him. "All I'm interested in is getting out of here and on my way home."

Romero left the room and closed the door behind him. She stared down at her newly manicured hands. Part of the polish had begun to chip. "Damn," she said.

Chapter Forty-Seven

J OINED BY JEMIMAH, Detective Romero stood in the hallway observing the witness through the one-way glass.

"Man, she's one tough cookie," he said.

Jemimah nodded. "Most psychopaths are. She believes she's smarter than law enforcement and that she's going to walk out of here scot-free. This is also training in Sociopath 101. They will not crack and will deny whatever evidence you confront them with."

Romero pressed one fist into the other. "We have more than enough evidence to present to the DA. I need her to admit she killed him. Otherwise a good defense attorney can break down all our evidence and call it circumstantial."

"She's a narcissist. You need to piss her off royally. All psychopaths have emotional triggers. You need to find one, then give it all you've got," Jemimah said.

While Jemimah and Detective Romero were engrossed in conversation, Tim McCabe walked over to the evidence room. Something had been gnawing at him all afternoon and this was an opportunity to confirm his suspicions. He signed in with the clerk at the front desk and checked the log to determine the ID number and location of the case files pertaining to the homicide. The clerk directed him to a section on the west side of the room.

Boxes were stacked on shelves in neat rows against the walls. McCabe located the file marked with the case number and pulled the cardboard box labeled *Victim's Hotel Room* down from the shelf, carried it to a table near the corner and began to remove the contents, stacking them neatly, one by one. He read the notes attached which listed the contents removed from the hotel room, including various and sundry items usually provided by motels, small bottles of shampoo and creams, bottled water, etc., all processed for prints.

He donned plastic gloves and continued to mull through the contents of the boxes, refilling each box as he emptied another. Then something caught his eye at the bottom of the last box. It was the telephone from the victim's room which had been on the night stand near the bed. He reached down into the box and pulled it out. Neatly wrapped in clear plastic, he unwrapped the phone and looked it over. The phone had an old fashioned answering machine powered by batteries, which were still intact. He flipped the top lid open to reveal a cassette recording tape still in place. As he closed the lid, the red light flashed, indicating Tanner had probably not listened to the messages. There was no indication in the notes that the techs had noticed the tape.

McCabe pressed the play button. On the first message, the front desk confirmed the victim's wake-up call for the next morning. And then on the second message, catching McCabe off guard, a woman's voice shrieked through the room.

He rewound the message and recorded it onto his phone. Noting the time as the day before the murder. He texted a message to Romero and attached the audio. He replaced the items in the evidence box and returned it to the shelf. On his way out, he signed out and thanked the clerk.

Romero looked up as McCabe walked toward him.

"How's it going, Rick?"

"Rough. Jemimah and I were just discussing that. I need

something to tip her over the edge."

"I think I have exactly what you need," McCabe said.

"What?"

"I just sent it to your phone."

Romero's phone vibrated, indicating a text was coming through. He pulled the message up and as he listened to the audio, a big smile crossed McCabe's face.

Romero patted him on the back. "Good work there, Tim. Come on, let's wrap up this charade."

He pushed on the door to the interrogation room and Eliza Simpson reached for her purse.

"Are we done here? I think I've had enough of this, Detective. You can contact me at my home number, which I'm sure you have in your file."

She stood to walk out. He motioned for her to sit down.

"I have just a couple more things I need to go over. Please, have a seat," Romero said.

She lowered herself into the chair. "Can you turn up the heat? It's freezing in here," she complained.

"Sorry, the thermostat is centrally controlled. I brought you some coffee. Maybe that will help," Romero said.

She stirred the packets of sweetener into the Styrofoam cup and took a sip. "Thank you. Now, why do you continue to drag this on?"

"Miss Simpson, as you are aware, we've spent a lot of time working on solving your fiancé's murder."

"What does that have to do with me? You have your suspect in jail. Isn't that enough?"

"A few things surfaced recently that need clarification," Romero said.

She sighed loudly. "Again, what does that have to do with me?"

"We're just looking for answers."

"I don't know any more than I've already told you."

Romero pulled up a chair across from her. "I am aware you've answered many questions in the interviews our department conducted, but these are matters which have come up and need clarification. All right?"

She pouted. "All right, if it will get me out of here sooner."

"What have you been doing since you've been in Santa Fe?"

"Waiting for word that my fiancé's body has been released. For God's sake, I didn't know there was so much red tape involved. I've lost a whole week of work, and now I need to get home and make final arrangements. Lawrence would have wanted me to do that." She produced a tissue from her pocket and dabbed at her eyes.

Romero continued. "Did you have plans to break up with Mr. Tanner before he traveled to New Mexico?"

"Of course not. That's ridiculous. We were going to be married. He was the man of my dreams. Why would I want to hurt him?" She reared her head. "Are you trying to get me to say *I* killed him? Is that what this is about? You people are grasping for straws. You have your killer. Jason Hodge killed Lawrence because he was coming back to convince his ex-wife to reconcile with him," she said.

"Didn't you say Lawrence had no intention of doing that?" Romero said. "Was it that you couldn't handle that he loved someone else?"

Simpson exploded. "You don't know what you're talking about!"

"Were you jealous because Brigid Tanner was so beautiful and he never stopped talking about her? Or was it true that maybe he really didn't love you?" Romero continued.

She slammed her fist on the table. "You have no idea!"

"Well, tell us, Eliza. Surely there's a reasonable explanation for all this," Romero said.

"You're damn right there is. I wasted over a year of my life putting up with this sniveling coward and listening to him piss and moan about how this woman had done him wrong."

Flustered and exasperated, she stood up. "Are we done now?"

"No, ma'am. We are not. Please sit down," he said, "or we'll have to restrain you."

She hugged herself and faced him. Her eyes flashed. "Why would I kill him? I loved him."

Romero could tell she was getting rattled. "Tell me a little about Lawrence. Was he a player?"

"What? Of course not."

"Were you angry at him because he was reluctant to make a commitment because he still had feelings for Brigid Hodge?"

She pretended to ignore the question. Romero repeated it.

"Consider this scenario. "Lawrence wanted to explore the possibility of reuniting with his ex. He wanted to postpone your wedding. You lost it, and in a moment of heated passion, you killed him."

"Bull. There's no truth to that and you know you can't prove anything," she said. "You're just a bunch of hicks looking for someone to pin this on."

Romero smiled. "This is nothing like what you see on TV," he said. "Contrary to what you may think, our Sheriff's Department is very thorough. In fact, in addition to all the other evidence against you, our crime lab conducted a search of your motel room. They not only discovered a pair of women's shoes in the trash, but also that the yellow hand towels provided with the room are identical to the one used to wrap the murder weapon found at the Hodge compound. The shoes, which we assume are yours, are being tested for the same residue found on those of the victim. I wouldn't be surprised if the tests will show them to be identical."

Eliza was silent. "You can't prove those are my shoes."

He reached into his shirt pocket. "Oh, another thing. You might want to listen to this." He placed his iPhone on the table in front of her and pressed the *play* icon. Her voice filled the room.

"Lawrence, I am so damned irritated that you haven't taken a minute to return any of my calls. I'm on my way there and don't try to tell me that you're hanging around just for the scenery. I know your ex-wife lives in Santa Fe and you went

there specifically to see her and try to convince her to come back to you. Don't try to deny it. You've been lying to me all this time, and you're going to be sorry for it."

"If it's any comfort, your fiancé never heard your rant," Romero said.

Eliza Simpson's eyes remained glued straight ahead, her breath coming in short, almost inaudible gasps. She turned and stared wildly at Romero for a few seconds and then broke down in tears.

"All right, all right," she screamed. "I killed him. Is that what you wanted to hear? Well, there it is. And I'm not sorry." She glared at Romero. "And don't look at me that way. Lawrence was a weakling, and determined to destroy our relationship by going back to his ex-wife. Now he can rot in hell." She put her hands on her cheeks and continued to sob. Trails of makeup mixed with dark mascara ran down her face. Romero placed the tissue box on the table in front of her.

Chapter Forty-Eight

D ETECTIVE ROMERO GAVE Eliza Simpson a few minutes to compose herself. He handed her a bottle of water.

"Just for the record, would you mind telling us how this all unfolded? It might help us to understand what happened," he said, in a gentler tone. "Take your time. You'll feel better once it's all out in the open."

Eliza sniffled and wiped her eyes. In a voice much smaller than before, she described how that Friday morning, she had awoken at four o'clock. She took a leisurely shower, blew her hair dry and fastened a flowered clip on one side of her hair. She applied a dab of makeup and touched her long lashes with mascara, carefully replacing the cap. After a dab of pink gloss to her lips, she turned and walked across the room and lifted her suitcase to the bed. She selected a pair of dark jeans and a black turtleneck. Next, she slipped on a pair of sneakers, laced them up and stood up to take one last look in the mirror. She reached for the hoodie draped over the chair and tied it around her shoulders. Satisfied, she pulled her purse off the door knob and headed out the door.

"I drove down Cerrillos Road and turned into the restaurant lot adjoining the Holiday Inn where I knew Lawrence was staying. The previous evening I had watched him climb up the stairs to the second level of the hotel and enter the third room from the corner. At five thirty that morning, the sun wasn't up yet, so I relaxed back on the headrest and listened to a classical music station featuring an early morning symphony by Vivaldi. I remember closing my eyes for a few minutes and humming along with the music.

"Around six o'clock, I saw the door to the room open and watched him exit from the room, backpack in hand. I waited and saw that he was alone, so I watched as he walked over to the side parking lot, where he stopped next to a red Ford Focus, disabled the alarm and slid the backpack onto the rear seat. I watched as he pulled out onto Cerrillos Road and headed south, then waited a few minutes more and then proceeded in the same direction. Early morning traffic was light and I knew the red car wouldn't be hard to spot, so I followed a comfortable distance behind."

Romero interrupted. "Did you know where he was headed?"

"No, but from his appearance, I figured he was going for a hike," she said.

Romero couldn't help but notice how Simpson's demeanor had changed as she related the events. It was as though she was telling a story at the dinner table. She was animated, focused and relaxed describing the scenario in great detail. He urged her to continue.

"So right before the exit to Highway 14, I pulled in behind a truck hauling a load of wood. I followed the truck until Lawrence turned onto a dirt road so I pulled over to the side of the highway and waited as he continued forward, obviously ignoring the sign indicating it was a dead end."

"Did he see you at any time?" Romero said.

"No, I watched from the road through a set of small binoculars, as he drove across a small clearing and parked in the shade of a grove of trees. He got out of the car, put his stuff in the trunk, and with a small backpack and a long stick he walked toward an outcropping of boulders and disappeared into the foliage."

"What did you do then?" Romero said.

"I parked where I knew my car couldn't be spotted, and I hurried across the grove, sticking close to the edge of the trail. After hiking several miles on an upward slope, I saw him stop in the shade ahead to take a sip of water."

"What were your intentions at that moment, if you recall?" Romero said.

"I was going to talk to him. To make him listen to me. And then I remembered how determined he was to reconcile with his ex, and all that time I had wasted on him came flashing before me. He needed to be punished for that and I realized that might be my only chance. I reached for the pistol in the muff of my hoodie and approached quietly."

"Did you already have it in your mind to kill him?" Romero said.

"Not at first. But then it was as though I was in a trance. Without hesitation, I placed my finger on the trigger and depressed the safety button, discharging a round from the firearm. I had not anticipated the recoil, which almost knocked me over, and I quickly released my finger from the trigger. The sound of the brass cartridge hitting a nearby rock still echoes in my head. I expected that the recoil made me miss, but when I looked up I saw him fall backward onto a bed of leaves and branches. I realized what I had done and I ran toward him and knelt beside the body."

"What was your reaction, if I might ask?" said Romero.

"Oh, my God. The sudden realization that he was dead sent me into a panic. My heart was pounding and my hands were shaking. I could feel the adrenalin rushing through me at a break-neck speed. I was scared. I looked around to see if anyone might have heard the shot, then I spotted a set of car keys dangling from his backpack, grabbed them and hurried back to his rental."

"What did you intend to do?" Romero said.

"I wanted something to cover him. A blanket. Anything. I found a sleeping bag in the trunk. I stopped for a minute to again make sure no-one had heard the gunshot, and then scurried back to where he lay. I gently covered him with the sleeping bag."

"Can I ask why you felt the need to do that?" Romero said.

"His eyes were staring up at me, and somewhere I had read that vultures and coyotes could make short work of someone in that condition. The thought sickened me. I replaced the keys and then broke a branch from a tree and swished it on the ground to cover any tracks I might have left. Then I took off running in the direction of my vehicle."

"Where did you go then?" Romero said. "You still had the pistol in your possession? Out of curiosity, when did you have occasion to plant the weapon?"

"I was shaking so hard, I could barely drive the twenty miles to my hotel room, but I still had one last thing to do, take the gun and hide it in the shed at the Hodge compound. From my last visit, I knew they drove into town on Fridays for supplies and were usually gone for several hours. I had discovered a back road that led to the creek adjoining the property, and it was the perfect place from which to make sure the entire family was gone before I made my way to the shed."

Her pupils dilated, she looked up at him like a child who had just completed turning in her homework. "Can I go now?"

Romero had not one shred of sympathy for Eliza Simpson. In his eyes, she was nothing more than a cold-blooded killer who allowed her insecurities and jealousy to take over. He turned to McCabe. "Get her booked. We're done here."

He walked out into the hallway where Jemimah waited. She squeezed his hand as they walked out of the building in silence.

Chapter Forty-Nine

T HE FOLLOWING MONDAY, before taking off on their honeymoon, Jemimah stopped by her office to print out their boarding passes and make sure no new emergencies were going to interrupt the honeymoon this time. She had just finished printing when Katie tapped on the doorjamb.

"I know you're heading out, but there's someone to see you, Doc."

Jemimah glanced at her Daybook, a puzzled look crossed her face. "I don't have any appointments scheduled, Katie. Remember, I'm leaving on my honeymoon. Reschedule them for the week after we return."

The voice behind Katie was one Jemimah would have recognized anywhere. Her heart picked up a beat as she started to protest.

Jason Hodge walked into the room. "No, please, Jemimah. Just give me a few minutes. I'm afraid if I don't say all this now, I might never have another chance."

Jemimah took a deep breath as she faced him. "All right, come in."

He stood in front of her desk. "Do you mind if I sit down?" he said.

She motioned toward the chair, "Of course, please."

Seeing him in person was much different than the photo she had seen in the newspaper when he was first arrested. Standing before her was just an older version of the father she remembered, the tall, ruggedly handsome, perpetually suntanned man, the one who turned her family life upside down when he joined the FLDS and began applying their rules.

He interrupted her thoughts. "I'm sure you've had a lot of questions over the years, and maybe even more so recently. I'm here to answer them, Jemimah," he said. "Better still, just let me talk so I can cover everything I need to say. I am so sorry for what you endured as a child, for what my actions put you through and disturbed you so much that you felt the need to leave. I'm not making excuses, but I was young, a rebel filled with ideas of power and control and I didn't care who got hurt as long as everything went my way."

Jemimah looked straight at him. "Might I ask what changed?"

He shifted in the chair. "About a year after you took off, it wasn't too long before your brother picked up and did the same thing. He left a letter and said a lot of things that opened my eyes. He said he couldn't respect a man who supported a leader whose morals and teachings were questionable, someone who imagined himself as a god and made self-serving decisions and tried to convince his followers it was for their better good."

"I'm sorry to hear that," Jemimah said. "I often wondered what had become of him."

"Your brother was very sad about your leaving. He looked up to you, and at some point he decided if you were brave enough to leave, then he was too. My greatest shame was that I had failed you two as a parent. I set unreachable standards and ridiculous rules which were impossible to adhere to. I hope you will be able to forgive me for ruining your childhood," he said, as his eyes misted.

Jemimah sighed. "You may have made my childhood years difficult, but leaving the group gave me a new life, one that I would have never had if I'd stayed. I couldn't imagine myself married at such a young age without ever having been able to pursue an education. It may have been a challenge, but I managed to survive," she said.

"That's one of the many things I came here to apologize for. I know I can't ever make it up to you, but I do want you to know that I have thought long and hard over the years, and knowing that you managed to survive on your own is such a relief to your mother and myself. It took a huge amount of courage and determination on your part.

"I've made mistakes in my life, but I've always tried to do what's right. Sometimes life is complicated, but that's no excuse. Change has come slowly, and I can only hope I'm a better man because I embraced a different set of principles than I started with. I have loved my wives and all my children, including you, Jemimah. I hope you know that."

He clasped his hands over his chest and continued. "We never gave up on seeing you again someday. I met your husband, Rick, and even if it was under pretty unfavorable circumstances, he seems to be a good man. We're happy for you. He says you were responsible for putting all the pieces together that led to my release."

"It's part of my job," she said. "I'm just sorry you had to spend all that time in jail, but as you know, the wheels of justice turn a bit slowly, especially up in the mountains."

"It was the first time in my life I've ever been confined like that, but it sure gave me a lot of time to think. In my heart I knew there would be a light at the end of the tunnel, and that turned out to be you, Jemimah. I can't thank you enough."

Jemimah took a deep breath. Her heart was filled with love and admiration for her father.

"You turned out to be so much more than I would have ever imagined, and I want you to know how proud I am to be your father. I hope sometime in the future you can see yourself clear to maybe spending some time with us, even if it's on the phone." He paused. "That's all I came here to say."

Jemimah didn't know what to say. Her first instinct had been to close her mind to anything he said, but part of her was relieved that she no longer had to hold anything in. For some reason, she wasn't able to express the anger she held for all these years. She could see that it would serve no purpose in doing so. Suffice it to say, a burden had been lifted from her shoulders. She declined to pass judgment on his circumstances, understanding it was a lifestyle he and the others had chosen.

She laid her hands palm down on the desk. "Thank you. That sums it up for me. I hold no animosity toward you and I appreciate that you thought enough of me to come here to make amends. That means a lot," she said.

He lowered his eyes. "I'm touched that you were willing to hear me out. We're moving back to Hildale in a few weeks and probably won't get another chance to see you. The movers are coming to pack things up. Byron Mills has listed the property and he's pretty confident we should have a buyer soon." He stood and leaned toward her. "This might be my only opportunity to ask. Could I have a hug?"

Jemimah choked back the emotions that had been waiting to erupt. "Yes, of course." She moved toward him. All the years of wishing and waiting for her father to express his feelings had just disappeared. They embraced for a long time. Jason Hodge then held his daughter at arm's length. "You must know how proud I am of you."

She nodded and smiled as he kissed her on the forehead. "I won't forget you, Jemimah. You'll always be in my heart."

Chapter Fifty

JEMIMAH WAS STILL misty-eyed when Romero greeted her at the bottom of the steps. He held out his hand.

"I was beginning to worry, you were taking so long. Is everything okay, Sweetie?"

She touched his cheek. "Yes, it is now."

He kissed her gently on the lips and kept his arms wrapped around her for a long moment.

She looked up at him, her eyes sparkling. "Let's get this honeymoon on the road, Detective. Oh, and one more thing. Don't you dare answer your phone!"

About Marie
Romero Cash

Marie Romero Cash is a mystery writer/artist based in
Santa Fe, New Mexico, the heart of the southwest.

Website: marieromerocash.com

www.ingramcontent.com/pod-product-compliance
Lightning Source LLC
Chambersburg PA
CBHW011118100726
47898CB00011B/3135